Born in the UK, **Becky Wicks** has suffered interminable wanderlust from an early age. She's lived and worked all over the world, from London to Dubai, Sydney, Bali, NYC and Amsterdam. She's written for the likes of *GQ*, *Hello!*, *Fabulous* and *Time Out*, a host of YA romance, plus three travel memoirs—*Burqalicious*, *Balilicious* and *Latinalicious* (HarperCollins, Australia). Now she blends travel with romance for Mills & Boon and loves every minute! Tweet her @bex_wicks and subscribe at beckywicks.com.

Also by Becky Wicks

Tempted by Her Hot-Shot Doc

Discover more at millsandboon.co.uk.

FROM DOCTOR TO DADDY

BECKY WICKS

MILLS & BOON

Published in Great Britain 2019
by Mills & Boon, an imprint of HarperCollins*Publishers*
1 London Bridge Street, London, SE1 9GF

© 2019 Becky Wicks

ISBN: 978-0-263-07975-3

MIX
Paper from
responsible sources
FSC™ C007454

This book is produced from independently certified FSC™ paper
to ensure responsible forest management.
For more information visit www.harpercollins.co.uk/green.

Printed and bound in Great Britain
by CPI Group (UK) Ltd, Croydon, CR0 4YY

PROLOGUE

FRASER STOPPED TO rest his arms on the ledge at the top of Edinburgh Castle. Brick houses, trees, and in the distance sparkling water shone like a painting under a clear blue sky. He inhaled a lungful of fresh Scottish air. The city was so damn beautiful when the sun shone.

The surgery was crazy, as usual, and he'd taken a morning walk to prep himself, but someone needed him already. He could tell by the vibrations in his pocket.

He pulled out his phone, turning his face to the rare sun. 'Hi, Anton.'

'Fraser, good morning. I came across a file that might be of interest for the *Ocean Dream*, if you're still looking for a dialysis nurse.'

'I am.' Fraser smiled at two kids running around a cannon, pretending to shoot each other.

He couldn't really remember which positions had been filled and which hadn't—he'd been so busy. In truth, he hadn't had time to think much about working on the cruise ship at all this year. That was why he'd put Anton in charge of recruiting the medical team.

'I've found a great dialysis nurse in London who fits the bill. But—get this. She *also* has a five-year-old daughter who's on the kidney donor list. Rare blood type. The kid's never been on a ship before, so naturally I thought...'

'Sounds great.' Fraser held the phone closer as the kids ran shrieking around him. He really needed all this in an email, otherwise he'd forget, but he asked anyway. 'What's

the nurse's name?' He started walking across the court towards the gate.

'Her name is Sara…'

Anton paused, obviously to look at something.

'Sara Cohen—and her kid's name is Esme.'

Fraser stopped abruptly and gripped the phone tight in his
hand. A tourist almost walked into the back of him.

'Sara Cohen?' The name brought a thin sheen of sweat to
his forehead. The cool breeze blew over it, giving him goose
bumps. How long had it been since he'd heard that name?
Six years? After a while he'd stopped counting.

He mouthed an apology to the lady he'd stopped in front
of. Her eyes swept his tall frame, in jeans, a fitted shirt and
blazer, and she blushed.

He stepped aside. 'Anton, when is the cruise, exactly—
remind me?'

'A month from today,' Anton said. 'Her daughter is pretty
pumped for it, as you can imagine. Sara's just waiting on the
go-ahead from St Gilda's, where she works, but between you
and me I think we've found our fit.'

Fraser's head was still reeling. *Sara Cohen had a five-
year-old daughter?* Maybe it was a different Sara Cohen.
'What's her background?

He forced his legs to continue down the hill, through the
crowds of tourists, past the bagpipe player in his kilt at the
bottom.

Anton described the nurse's profile, some of which he
knew, some of which he didn't. It was definitely the same
Sara Cohen.

Six years had come between them. Six years of no
contact… Aside from that one time he'd flown to London to
talk to her and seen her with that other guy. The sight had
made his insides burn. He'd regretted going there instantly,
and hadn't attempted contact with her since. Not that she'd
made any attempt with him either.

'What about the father?' he said now, trying not to sound as if he was fishing. 'Esme's father—Sara's husband?'

'It'll just be the two of them,' Anton said. 'She's single, as far as I know.'

In the car on his way to the surgery, Fraser's brain ran on overdrive. He could still see her face, standing in his bedroom, telling him they should go their separate ways. She'd never even let him have a say.

He could also vividly picture her standing with that guy, outside the restaurant at the end of her street. She'd been in a nurse's uniform. Had that been Esme's father? Why had he left them?

Think about this, he told himself sternly as he drove. He'd been about to cancel his work on the cruise—send someone else in his place. The Breckenridge Practice was busier than ever. Plus, living away from his mother in the new apartment still left him with enough of a twinge of guilt without him heading off to sea. His parents had run the practice from an extension of the huge family home for fifteen years. It still felt empty without his father.

But this was *Sara Cohen*. The woman he'd sworn six years ago he would one day make his wife.

Maybe he should rethink working on one more cruise.

CHAPTER ONE

No sooner had Sara heaved her suitcase onto her single bed and flung it open than a voice sounded out over the Tannoy, making her jump.

'Could all renal care specialists report on Deck One for orientation in five minutes' time? Thank you.'

She swept the back of her hand across her clammy brow and caught sight of herself in the tiny mirror, visible through the open bathroom door. Calling it a bathroom was a stretch, and already a source of amusement. She'd never been in a bathroom that looked this much like a cupboard before.

Running the tap and splashing cold water onto her face, she considered that she shouldn't have taken that call from her father back at the hotel, which in turn had caused them to board the *Ocean Dream* at the very last minute. Now she had barely any time to change before she was due upstairs to join Esme and her new on-board carers, plus all the other patients she'd be sailing through the Caribbean with.

'Anything can happen at sea. You'd better look after each other.'

She recalled the gentle warning in her father's words. She hoped he needed no real reassurance that Esme would be fine. She was in her care after all.

She also hoped Esme wasn't too scared, up on deck. This was a big deal for a five-year-old—let alone one like Esme. Not only was this the first time she'd been on a ship, or a boat of any kind, it was her first time away from the dialysis clinic.

She hurried to reapply her lipstick in the tiny mirror.

Esme was the lucky one here, really. She got to share a big cabin on another floor with several other kids—like a giant fun sleepover, complete with two carers on shift at all times. Sara was going to have to work night shifts, so sharing a cabin with her daughter just wouldn't have been an option.

Applying her mascara, she thought of her sister, and their conversation the night before they'd left London for Fort Lauderdale.

'I still can't believe you're working on a cruise. I thought you hated the ocean,' Megan had said.

'I don't *hate* the ocean. You *think* I hate the ocean because I didn't want to go snorkelling with you and your Latino lover. You were all over each other out there—I'm surprised the fish didn't throw up.'

They'd laughed, but they'd both known it was still a bit of a sore point that their last 'girls' holiday' together—almost a year ago now—had wound up with Megan frolicking in the waves for a week with a Mexican guy called Pedro, while Sara read the entire *Game of Thrones* series on her sun-lounger, feeling guilty about leaving Esme.

'It's not for pleasure this time anyway—it's for work.'

'I know…' Megan had sighed.

Megan knew all about the haemodialysis patients, of course, and how much Sara cared for every single one in her charge.

If it hadn't been for Esme's illness, Sara would probably never have thought about adding dialysis training to her medical repertoire, but she was thankful now, more than ever, that she had.

'Can you believe I get to introduce her to this new world, Megan? I get to help *all* these people see places they never thought they'd see.'

'I think it's amazing, what you're doing,' her sister had told her sincerely. 'But just make sure you have some fun yourself this time, OK?'

'I know, I know.'

The dialysis care was just part of Sara's new position on the ship. She'd been hired as a member of the *Ocean Dream*'s wider medical team.

While she'd signed up for Esme's benefit, and for whomever else might need her expertise on-board, she knew that during their free periods the ship's staff were permitted to hang out on the main deck, where a lot of activities were set to take place.

They would be able to mingle with the guests and even go shore-side if the ship was in port. It was pretty much all-expenses-paid travel with a salary on top, and an opportunity she hadn't been able to refuse when that nice recruitment guy Anton had called.

Draping her ship ID on its lanyard around her neck, she hurried out of the cabin and made her way down the narrow corridor to the elevator, smoothing her blonde shoulder-length waves of hair as she went.

She observed again the opulence of the ship. Paintings depicting landscapes and seascapes hung on the walls of the dark wood-panelled corridors. The golden railings beneath them warned of potential bumpy waters. But she was more excited than nervous.

The *Ocean Dream*'s dialysis team involved a handful of dedicated professionals from the UK, who would be caring for individuals on dialysis. Most of their patients were travelling with their families from Port Everglades.

She'd been told some of the regular medical staff on board rotated around various ships throughout the season. It sounded like a fascinating lifestyle. But for her this was a one-off. She could never contemplate it long term while she had Esme's illness and her schooling to contend with.

'It's so fancy, isn't it?' An elderly lady giggled as she passed a painting of a golden-tailed mermaid.

'It's "a five-star hotel on the ocean",' Sara replied, quoting the website and hurrying on towards the upper deck, her green summer dress swishing at her ankles.

Passengers were still wheeling cases into staterooms on both sides of her and she felt another spike of exhilaration. The *Ocean Dream* was a luxurious beast, packed with almost five thousand regular customers, all paying top coin for, also quoting the website, *A unique combination of first-class accommodation, live entertainment, exceptional cuisine and a wide choice of restaurants, bars, lounges and clubs.*

Bermuda, Aruba and Antigua were all on the itinerary. And Sara was still grinning at the prospect of introducing Esme to the joys of sandcastle-building in the Caribbean when she reached the deck.

The harsh Florida sun launched at her head and shoulders, blinding her for a moment to the crowd gathered round a makeshift stage where Dr Renee Forster, the highly regarded leader of the dialysis team and one of the two practising nephrologists on board, was already speaking.

'Sorry I'm late,' she whispered to Esme's official carer, Jess.

Esme, standing at her knee height in denim shorts and a purple T-shirt, seemed concerned.

Sara took her little fingers. 'How are you doing, baby girl?'

Esme shrugged at the floor.

'We're so excited to have you all on board today!' Dr Forster, a tall African American woman with a hard New York accent, was beaming. 'As you can see, the weather is perfect, and our captain assures me that our departure and our days at sea en-route to Aruba will be plain sailing. Plenty of time for us all to get to know each other.'

Sara squeezed Esme's small hand reassuringly. She looked around her. It seemed her own daughter was set to be her youngest dialysis patient, which wasn't unusual.

Perspiring porters in white and blue uniforms were still loading crates and bags and boxes from ramps onto the ship. Palm trees were waving from the port like jealous passengers.

She noticed a kid in green board shorts far across the deck—not part of their group. He was whispering something to his mother, who looked away quickly when Sara met her eyes.

Instincts primed, she knew the young boy had been asking about the bandage over Esme's catheter, poking out above the neckline of her T-shirt. It was either that or the camcorder Esme wouldn't put down. It was practically glued to her hand these days.

'What a ship, huh?' she whispered, concerned that her sweet daughter might see the boy and feel embarrassed. Esme was already more than aware of how different she was from other children. 'Are you as excited as me right now?'

Esme just shrugged again. Something twisted in Sara's gut. It wasn't straightforward, bringing a kid on dialysis on holiday.

Dr Forster was still speaking. 'Remember, our nurses are experienced, licensed dialysis nurses, so you're in good hands. We're all here to ensure your exact dialysis prescriptions are met, and also that your special dietary needs are accommodated with the help of the ship's dining staff. That's them over there.'

Sara turned to where she was pointing. The line-up of catering staff raised their hands in greeting. They scanned the faces of the roughly twenty patients they'd be caring for, their eyes all lit up in excitement.

'I'd like to take this opportunity to introduce the wonderful Dr Fraser Breckenridge, our Chief Doctor and Head of the *Ocean Dream*'s Medical Department. He'll be overseeing all the medical issues aboard the ship, so chances are you'll see him around. Can you come up here for a second, Dr Breckenridge?'

Sara blinked. Maybe she'd misheard.

No, she hadn't misheard.

Time stopped and then started moving backwards.

Fraser Breckenridge, in all his gym-honed glory, was striding from her vivid memory bank, right into her present. She watched in shock as he took his place on the stage.

It can't be...

Dr Forster handed him a microphone. Sara scanned his muscled six-foot-three frame as his presence immediately dominated not just the stage, but the entire deck of the ship. It was really him. *Why?* And why did he have to look so good?

She couldn't help but stare. From where she was standing he looked exactly as he had the night she'd left him in his giant family home that doubled as the Breckenridge Practice in Edinburgh. She hadn't heard from him since—not that she blamed him for that entirely. She'd never thought she'd see him again.

She considered sneaking away from the orientation, but Esme still had hold of her hand. Besides, the second Fraser's thick, unmistakably Scottish accent filled the air with its sticky heat, her legs turned to jelly. God, she had loved this man. Just the sound of his voice brought it all rushing back.

'Thank you so much, ladies and gents,' he said with gravelly familiarity, towering over Dr Forster in spite of her own height, and sweeping a big hand through his mane of thick black hair.

Sara could picture his eyes too, up close, and the honest blue of them she'd been happy to swim in for hours. She swallowed as the deck seemed to close in on her.

'I'm privileged to be able to join you on this special adventure. I know that for some of you this is the first time you'll have been on a ship—am I right? Who's never been on a ship before?'

To Sara's surprise, Esme released her grip on her and raised her hand tentatively. Her throat dried up as Fraser's eyes travelled to her daughter and then landed right on *her*. A tiny trail of perspiration began its descent down her lower back. She raised her hand at him slowly, in greeting. He did the same—like a Martian making contact with another planet. A flicker of a smile crossed his lips.

'Well, it looks like we're going to have some fun on this cruise,' he said, after a pause.

Sara wasn't entirely sure if he was still talking to Esme, or to her. She was picturing his lips now, too. The way they'd used to seem to melt against hers.

She hadn't read the staff list. She kicked herself. She'd had every intention of running her eyes over it, along with the plethora of other information she'd been sent, but Esme had been in a panic over a missing shoe when it had arrived in her inbox and she'd been side-tracked.

'Let me tell you: this weather is a tad nicer than it is in Edinburgh right now. I hope you won't be too horrified if this pale white Scottish skin turns as red as a lobster's!'

Esme giggled at Fraser's words, as did most of the crowd. Sara just felt hot and bothered. She was back in that huge Scottish house now, standing stunned on the stairs, hearing his father tell Fraser what he really thought about their six-month relationship, hearing Fraser do *nothing* to defend it—or her. They hadn't known she'd been listening.

Fraser was still talking, introducing the other staff—introducing *her*. 'Please also welcome Sara Cohen, one of our excellent dialysis nurses.'

She tried not to flinch as everyone turned to her and applauded, while Esme leaned into her shyly, clutching her camera. Annoyance was quickly overriding shock.

How dared he rock up here, on *her* adventure, six years after he'd let her go? OK, so she'd chosen to end their relationship herself that night, after overhearing their little family conversation. But if she hadn't done it Fraser would only have done it himself. She'd simply been saving him the bother and herself the heartbreak.

She hadn't needed any more heartbreak back then. Her mother had just died and her father had completely fallen apart. She'd been exhausted from taking care of him, all whilst dealing with her own grief. She'd been at Fraser's place for the weekend to cry in his arms, to let someone take care of *her* for a while. And then...

'Now, I'm sure you're all excited to get going and see what's planned for you. I'll hand you over to our events co-ordinator to tell you more.'

Fraser still had the audience enchanted.

'I'm looking forward to getting to know some of you over the next few weeks—although, let's be honest here, most people seem to have a better time on this ship if they never get to see me at all, if you know what I mean!'

Jess took Esme's other hand. 'Ready to meet the other kids?' she asked her daughter cheerily.

Sara dropped a kiss on Esme's cheek. Her heart was thudding as they walked away. A guy with a topknot called Tony was already on the stage, talking of tropical island walks and buffet lunches. And Fraser was heading straight through the crowd towards her.

She turned quickly towards the exit. She needed space to think. Maybe she and Esme could transfer ships. There was another one leaving in a few days' time; perhaps they could switch and avoid this. It was the last thing she needed— dredging up her painful past in the middle of the ocean, with no escape.

'Sara Cohen! Come on—don't walk away from me, lass.'

Fraser's voice was a powerful lasso, stopping her in her tracks. She closed her eyes as her hand found the smooth cool steel of the door handle. *So surreal.*

'After all this time,' he said, putting a big hand to her shoulder and causing goosebumps to flare on her hot skin. 'Weren't you even going to say hello?'

CHAPTER TWO

'WHAT ARE YOU doing here?'

'You didn't know I'd be on board?' He ran his eyes over her green dress, noting the way it nipped in at her slender waist. She'd barely put on a pound. In fact, maybe she'd even lost weight. Her bronzed cheekbones were sharper than he remembered. Perhaps her hair was shorter...

She bit her lip. He still remembered the feel of his tongue running along that lip.

'I can't do this,' she said. 'Please, Fraser, not here.'

She turned from him quickly again, pulled the door open and headed down the top floor corridor of the ship.

He followed her and caught her arm gently. 'Sara, come on.' He forced his voice to remain calm. 'Can we go somewhere and talk?'

A look of discomfort verging on pain flashed across her features before she pulled away from him. 'I don't know what's going on,' she said, standing against the wall in the corridor. 'But I'm here with my daughter and I'm here to work. This is just...' She folded her arms. Then she closed her eyes, appearing unnerved by his proximity. 'This is just not what I was expecting.'

'I'm sorry.' He stepped closer anyway, on the anchor-patterned carpet, till his feet were almost touching hers. 'I thought you knew I'd be here,' he said honestly. 'I assumed you'd have seen the list of medical staff and would have called me, or not taken the job if you had a real problem with it.'

He could smell her perfume—different from the one he remembered. It was like an extra layer to her he'd never known, and it served to widen the gap that had clearly grown between them over the years.

'How would I have called you?' she challenged him. 'I don't have your number any more.'

'I never changed it. You also know where I work. Remember? It's the house you walked out of with no credible explanation?'

Flecks of amber flickered around her pupils, launching him straight back to those nights when he'd spent for ever just lying in bed next to her, observing the colours in her eyes.

'Well, maybe I would have tried calling you if I'd known what was coming,' she said. 'But for now I suppose I should just try and transfer ships. If you'll excuse me?'

She continued towards the elevator at the end of the corridor. He followed her. He hadn't expected that. 'Cohen, we need to talk about this like adults.'

'Why?'

Her arms were still folded as she waited for the elevator. She scanned his tall frame as she dug her own nails into her flesh, exhaling a harried sigh.

'Fraser, seriously, what are you *doing* here? Aren't you supposed to be running the Breckenridge Practice in Edinburgh?'

'Things change.' He lowered his voice. This wasn't the place to explain about that.

A voice called out behind him. 'Watch out, mister!'

'Sorry, man!' Fraser had almost caused a deck hand to crash into them. The young lad was carrying a heavy crate of what looked like fruit towards them.

Pulling Sara against the wall with him, to make room, Fraser covered her hand with his against the smooth wooden wall and squeezed it tight.

'God, I've missed you,' he found himself saying. 'I like your hair like that.'

He swore he felt her shiver. For a second he saw a glimmer of the old her, the way she'd been before she'd taken it upon herself to end things just six months after they'd started something really good. The last time they'd exchanged any words at all she'd been just twenty-five, and he twenty-six.

'Let's go somewhere and clear the air,' he said, seizing his chance as the elevator doors opened. 'Sara, you never really let me have my say back then. I understand you were grieving for your mother, but a lot was going on and—'

'A lot is going on *now*,' she said.

Her walls were back up, clearly.

'Listen, I'm getting my stuff, then I'm going to see if Esme and I can be put on another cruise. This is beyond unprofessional Fraser. What makes you think you can trap me on a ship and tell me you've missed me, and expect me to just—'

'*Trap* you on a ship?' He smiled in spite of it all. The door shut behind them. The deckhand pressed the button reading 'Deck Four' with his elbow, still holding the crate. 'I would never trap you anywhere, Sara. I let you go six years ago, didn't I?'

She chewed on her cheek, looking at the floor. 'We let each other go, Fraser. The past is the past and it's where it should stay. I have Esme to think about now.'

'I never even knew you had a daughter.'

'She was a surprise for me, too.'

He frowned internally at this new information. 'I'm so sorry—about the dialysis, I mean.'

'We don't need your pity.'

'That's not what I...' He shut his mouth, seeing she was clearly uncomfortable. Almost as uncomfortable as the deck hand, now staring at his crate. What a tragedy for the family, though—as if Sara losing her mother hadn't been tragic enough.

Sara had been inconsolable after her mother had died. It had been extremely sudden. Cancer, stage three, terminal.

After it had happened he'd flown to London to be with her. He'd skipped classes and his duties to stay beside her, then he'd invited her back to Scotland.

His father had been less than impressed.

He'd been under so much pressure back then, to help his parents secure the future of the practice. Remodelling had been needed, and new equipment, more staff. They'd needed money—*his* money, from the family trust fund.

He'd been juggling extra studies with extra work for his father, in order to qualify faster, when Sara had ended their relationship out of nowhere, citing the need to focus on her own family back in London. When she'd left him it had hit him like an avalanche.

The elevator doors were flung open. The deck hand shuffled off with his crate, without a word.

'Stop following me,' Sara huffed as he followed her down the corridor. She swiped her ID, which doubled as a key card, and went to shut the cabin door after herself.

He was ready for it. He wedged a foot in the door to stop it closing. 'Have you thought about Esme upstairs, all excited about this trip, while you're down here thinking about leaving? 'We have a job to do, here, Cohen.'

'Have I thought about Esme? She is *all* I think about!'

He regretted his words. 'I'm sorry. I just… God, woman, just let me in.'

She tutted loudly as she moved from blocking the door, and he squeezed into the cabin after her.

Looking around, he let out a small laugh that he stifled before she got even more annoyed. '*This* is where they put you?'

'Why? Where did they put *you*?' Sara looked confused now, forgetting her anger for a second.

He bit his tongue. It probably wasn't the best time to tell her that he'd been given a double suite all to himself. He had a leather couch, a balcony, a mini-bar and a TV, complete with a shelf full of DVDs. One of them was *Titanic*. He couldn't imagine anyone watching *Titanic* on a cruise ship…

Sara was gathering up items from the tiny bathroom to put in her suitcase. 'Wow… OK, Cohen, you're serious.'

'Stop calling me that.'

'I always call you that—it's your name, isn't it? Unless you're married.' He feigned indifference. Anton had told him she was single—as far as he knew, at least.

'I'm not married,' she confirmed quickly. 'I never was. Esme's father is long gone.'

He saw her cast a glance to his finger—checking for a ring, perhaps?

'I've been too busy to date much, never mind get married. The practice takes a lot of work,' he explained.

'I'm sure it does. It always did.'

Her dig stung.

'Don't you think it will look a wee bit strange to our patients if one of their trusted dialysis nurses disembarks before we've even gone anywhere?' he pointed out. 'You've come a long way for this, Sara. You both have.'

Sara ignored him, though she'd started packing more slowly already. She knew she had no intention of leaving—not really. She was just feeling put on the spot, out of her depth.

'So, how long has Esme been on dialysis?' He lowered himself onto the single bed and noticed two knitting needles and a ball of red wool sticking out of the case before she pulled a sweater on top of them.

'Too long. She was eight months old when she got E. coli. It got worse and turned into HUS.'

'Haemolytic uremic syndrome?' He was well aware of how such a disease could destroy the kidneys.

'She's on the transplant list but there's never been a match for her. I tell her it's because she's special—which she is. She's so special that none of her family can help her with a new kidney.'

The tone of her voice made him reach a hand to her arm again, briefly. 'That must be tough, Sara.'

She studied his long fingers. 'It's OK. We live with Dad and he helps out at home. We have things under control... most of the time. So where exactly is *your* cabin, hotshot?'

She clearly wanted to change the subject. 'Hotshot?' he said out loud. Sara was pretty hot too, from what he remembered.

They'd met in Edinburgh, where she'd been in training for an advanced nursing degree. At the time he'd been in and out of St Enid's hospital, in his last year of a three-year residency, and he'd noticed her at first because of her knitting. Sara Cohen had knitted whenever she'd had a spare moment. Baby clothes, she'd told him later, on their first date, for the kids on the children's ward.

He'd only *really* taken notice of her that time in the treatment room, when she'd done some tests on him ahead of a marathon he'd been about to run. He recalled it again now—that day the sparks had first flown—and couldn't help smiling ruefully.

'My cabin's up on the second deck,' he told her, picturing them both in his bed as he said it. He couldn't help it.

The Tannoy cut in.

'Ladies and gentlemen, we'll be leaving port in approximately fifteen minutes. Please do join us on the top deck for your welcome drink and to wave goodbye to land for a couple of days. We wish you all a safe and happy journey!'

'I have to go.' Sara dragged her suitcase off the bed, narrowly missing his foot with it.

Fraser took it from her hands with ease. 'Give me a break, Cohen. You know you don't really want to go.'

'I told you to stop calling me that.'

She flung the cabin door open and heaved the suitcase from his hands, hauling it out into the corridor. She made it to the elevator again, panting, and pressed the button.

Part of him was impressed. 'You're seriously going to get off this ship? In front of everyone up there?' he asked in the elevator. The mirrors reflected an infinite number of Saras. He didn't miss her looking at him, though.

'Yes, Fraser, that is exactly what I'm going to do.'

'I can't wait to see this.' He could tell she thought she'd gone too far with her dramatics to back down now. As stubborn as ever.

Back on deck, he held his hand up to stop a porter rushing to help her. Esme wandered over to them. She was holding a camcorder. He noticed her catheter now, the pink of her cheeks.

'Well, hello again, you.' He bent down to her height, held out his hand. 'We never officially met.'

The kid had Sara's eyes—almond-shaped pools filled with questions. What kind of father would abandon his kid? He didn't know the full story, of course, but he couldn't imagine it was a happy one.

'Are you having fun?' he asked her.

'Kind of. What's my mum doing?'

Sara was trying her hardest to stop three men from pulling in a walkway that led down to the pier. Someone blew a whistle. People were waving goodbye to others below.

'Your mum's just processing some new information. She'll be fine. I see we have the ship's film-maker on board already. Have you got any good stuff yet, Miss Spielberg?'

She giggled. 'Some.'

'Maybe we can take you behind the scenes sometime? Show you the kitchens and the bridge?'

Her eyes lit up. 'Yes, please! Can I get some film of *you*?'

'Only if you capture my good side. Which side do you think that is?' He turned his head from side to side, pulling different faces as he did so, and Esme giggled again, her whole face lighting up.

From the corner of his eye he saw Sara watching them. He stood straighter and took Esme's little hand as the ship juddered. It was too late for her to make her exit.

'No luck? You can always swim for it,' he teased as she approached them.

She rolled her eyes, but he didn't miss the slight smile on her lips. Esme skipped off to view the ship's departure through the railings.

'Thanks for that—she seems a bit happier now, at least,' Sara said with a sigh.

Her green dress blew against his legs. 'She's going to have a great time,' he assured her.

'She's bullied, you know. The kids call her names because of the central line in her neck. I got her the camera so she could make a video diary—show people she can live a normal life, doing stuff like this. I thought she could put it on her donor page.'

Sara swept her blonde hair behind her ears, following Esme with her eyes. Fraser thought again how messed up it was that they hadn't found a donor for her yet. 'That's a great idea.'

'I don't want anything to ruin this trip for Esme, Fraser.'

'Neither do I.'

'What's this doing here?' Dr Renee Forster had walked over and was pointing down at Sara's suitcase in the middle of the deck. 'Everything OK?'

'She spilled some water on it downstairs,' Fraser said quickly. 'She thought the sun would dry it off faster.'

Sara held up her hands. 'Silly me. But it worked; it's already dry.'

Renee raised her eyebrows. 'I see. Good to have you both on board. You know each other well, I take it?'

'We did a long time ago.'

Sara shifted uncomfortably on the spot and he tried not to smirk.

'We dated for six months, actually,' he said. 'We're in a kind of the-one-that-got-away situation.'

Sara turned to him in shock, but he shrugged his shoulders. Staff on these cruises had no secrets. And anything that needed to be addressed was bound to come out, one way or another.

As the ship finally pulled away to the cheers of the crowd, the thought made him anxious almost as much as it thrilled him.

CHAPTER THREE

'CAN I HAVE pizza tonight?' Esme asked. 'Because we're on holiday?'

Sara finished unhooking her daughter from the dialysis machine. 'Sorry, sweetie, but you already know that's not a good idea. Your diet should stay the same, so you're not poorly.'

Esme groaned and laid her head down heavily on the pillow.

'I know it's hard,' Sara sympathised. 'There's a lot of great food on this ship.'

That was an understatement. The food on the *Ocean Dream* was unlike anything she'd ever seen or tasted. Each buffet was like a dream, with everything from lobster sushi rolls to king crab soufflé, to marinated steaks and more cakes than she could count.

'If I can't have pizza, can I have ice-cream? Just a bit?'

Sara turned off the dialysis machine and readjusted the lines from Esme's catheter. 'We'll see. You *have* to stop pointing that thing at me!' She play-swiped at the camcorder lens that was pointed at her face.

'Dr Fraser doesn't mind being on camera.'

'Yes, well…'

Sara snapped off her gloves a little too loudly. She was burning to know more about Fraser—why he'd left the family practice, how often he did these cruises, whether he'd met anyone else since her. Especially that. But she didn't want

to appear as if she was invested in anything Fraser Breckenridge had going on any more.

She'd meant what she said. Esme came first. She was all
that mattered. Besides, they were professionals, and Renee
was already looking between them like Cupid eyeing up the
perfect target for an arrow.

Fraser had asked if they could talk privately once they
reached Aruba and left the ship. She'd refused, maintain-
ing she was there to concentrate on her work and Esme, not
dwell on their past relationship. But a mish-mash of memories had kept her up the last two nights—things she hadn't
thought about in years.

*'Code Blue. Is anyone close to the casino? Can we get
help in the casino, please?'*

The Tannoy was practically screaming. Jess stood up
from her chair in the corner. 'Code Blue in the casino? That's
just next door!'

'Take Esme to the playroom, will you?' Sara unhooked
another dialysis patient beside her and hurried outside.

The flashing lights and jingling slot machines in the ship's
casino launched an attack on her senses. She gripped her
Ocean Dream branded medical case harder as she started
down an aisle, waiting for her eyes to adjust.

'Sara! Over here.'

People were being ushered away by a security guard
wearing the ship's smart grey uniform. Fraser was crouched
on his haunches over a large balding gentleman in his mid
to late fifties.

'What happened?' She dropped to her knees beside him.
It could have been the sight of him, knee-deep in an emergency, but her heart immediately upped its pounding.

'Cardiac arrest. Help me intubate him. I've already called
for a stretcher.' He paused for a beat to meet her eyes. 'They
said he won some pretty big money. He obviously got so excited he collapsed.'

Sara felt stabs of adrenaline, as if she was hot-wired to

Fraser as he started CPR. Nosy onlookers in cruise ship attire and enough bling to sink the ship stood out against others who were happily still playing on the slot machines, only feet away.

She finished fixing the Ambu-bag and an oxygen cylinder, then quickly lifted out the nasal tubes. Fraser took over. His Adam's apple rose subtly above the collar of his white shirt and she followed it up to the dark line of stubble around his jaw as he pumped on the rich man's hairy, tanned chest. A Rolex watch caught her eye. A golden wedding band.

Fraser held the man's head back so she could help, and she lifted his puffy eyelids, noting the pale green irises. Behind her a slot machine dispensed more coins with a happy jingle. So bizarre.

She inserted the tube into the man's trachea slowly, while the efficient blur that was Fraser administered more CPR. His biceps flexed through his shirt. Sweat glistened on his neck. Someone was talking about a stretcher. It was close. But she could barely hear a thing against the pinging and spinning and chinking of the coins.

'Go again!'

Holding the man's head on her lap, she put two fingers to his neck as Fraser commenced with another set of compressions. His hair was falling almost into his steely blue eyes. He was completely focused.

She held her breath. Still no movement under her fingers. Fraser watched her shake her head and used the Ambu-bag for rescue breaths. Their shoulders were touching. A stretcher was being carried down the aisle.

'Everyone move aside, please. We have a medical emergency. Move aside, please.'

People responded quickly to Fraser, reading the waves of urgency in his words. Where was this man's wife? Sara wondered. Was she on board too? Maybe he'd come here without her? Lots of people came on cruises alone—some kind of escapism, she supposed, from whatever they hoped could be left on shore.

They lifted the man onto the stretcher together.

Was Fraser Breckenridge escaping something out here? He'd tried to call her after she'd left him six years ago, but she hadn't answered. When she'd fallen pregnant, after an out-of-character, grief-stricken, vodka-fuelled one-night stand, she'd seen it as one more sign that she and Fraser were truly over—especially when he'd stopped trying to contact her. Even if Fraser *had* wanted to be with her, there was no way she would have asked him to help raise another man's baby.

'Let's get him on life support,' Fraser said, jolting her back to the moment.

The medical centre, which was more like an infirmary, was located on the second deck. The smell of disinfectant was an extra punch to her swirling gut as they hurried in, and she clicked onto autopilot as they passed oxygen masks and pads and the IV.

Fraser arranged the patient on one of the few beds. It was just the two of them in the room. She started tugging the man's shirt open even further, noting the soft gleam on his bald forehead, the dents around his ears from his glasses. Where *were* his glasses?

She prepped him for the defibrillator, just as Fraser rushed to hook it up. She watched him administer the jolts at one-fifty, eyeing the defib screen for signs of life, and noticed, despite herself, the faint lines on Fraser's face that hadn't been there six years ago—extra layers of thought around his forehead.

There was still no pulse.

'Give me more,' he instructed.

She obeyed and prayed it would work. The room was getting hotter. It felt as if hours had passed in the tiniest space she'd ever had to work in, packed with lab test equipment, immobilisation boards, X-ray and EKG machines and bottle after bottle of pills. Through the window land was now in sight, shimmering green under bright sunshine.

It was still a whole new world to her. It clearly wasn't to Fraser.

'We have a pulse!' she announced finally, and relief flooded her veins.

A knock on the door minutes later made her jump, and she found her hand on Fraser's arm. He steadied her, and at his touch she felt something inside her waking from a deep slumber.

'Is he alive? Oh, God, please don't tell me he's dead. He always said he wanted to die on a cruise ship… He blimmin' well said that before we left…'

A busty, tanned woman was talking at the speed of an auctioneer as she tottered over on high heels and placed two leathery brown hands on their patient's cheeks, peering with squinty eyes into his big round face.

'He's breathing,' she stated.

Sara couldn't tell specifically if the woman thought that was a good thing or a bad thing.

'You'll be happy to know he has more than a few years left in him yet,' Fraser told her.

Sara watched the woman pull something from her glossy designer handbag. 'I'm so sorry, Harry. I was in the wine club with the ladies.' She placed a pair of glasses on his face before dropping a tender kiss on his forehead.

Maybe she really did love poor old Harry, Sara thought, glancing at Fraser, who promptly shot her a wink. Love wasn't always black and white, after all. Perhaps she should give Fraser a chance to say his piece. What had happened between them hadn't all been his fault, after all; maybe they owed it to each other at least to get the past out, so that they could put it behind them and work together without it hanging over them.

Right?

No. Bad idea.

Hearing Fraser explain himself might mean she'd open a door that was better off closed. No matter the attraction that would never go away, everything was different now. Esme needed her mother's full attention. What if they couldn't find a donor for her?

Oh, God, she couldn't lose Esme.

CHAPTER FOUR

'WHAT'S THAT THING stuck to your body?' The kid in the bright green board shorts was pointing a finger at Esme's catheter. 'Are you an alien?'

Fraser's brow creased where he sat three feet away on a beach chair, but Esme dropped the spade she was carrying and turned on her camcorder.

'What do you know about kidneys? Three, two, one—go!' She was challenging the kid, with five years of confidence behind her words. 'I bet you don't know *anything*.'

The boy's face scrunched up. He put a hand over the lens as his mother called out from beneath a giant sun hat in the shallows. 'Marcus! What are you doing?'

'You're weird,' Marcus told Esme loudly, and ran off.

Sara was off her chair in a flash.

'It's OK, Mummy.' Esme sounded tired. 'I know he just doesn't understand.'

'No, he doesn't.'

Fraser watched Sara reapplying her daughter's sunscreen, listened to her chatter, trying to make her smile. She made a great mother. He'd always known she would make a good mother, and there had been a time when he'd actually thought they'd make a great team as parents some day—not that he'd ever told her that.

Sara had her work cut out for her, though. Esme was smart and resilient and beautiful, and who knew her fate, exactly? Some people on dialysis lived a long time. Others didn't.

He stood and got them both to pose with their backs to

the ocean for a photo. Jess, the carer, took the camera and urged him into the shot.

'That's OK,' he told her, but Esme had other ideas.

'Dr Fraser, come and be in our photo!'

He waded into the shallows, eyes on Sara. Her expression gave nothing away. The hot sun was playing on her blue bikini top as Esme clung to their hands in the middle of them and demanded to be bounced up and down in the waves.

'Again!' she cried as they lifted her up and down.

'You're a bossy little Spielberg,' Fraser told her, picking her up and putting her on his shoulders in the surf. He pretended he was about to dunk her, lowering himself down into the water and then standing again quickly.

Esme screeched with laughter. When he caught her eye, Sara was laughing too.

'Where *is* this place?' Sara asked him later, taking his hand and letting him help her off the scooter he'd hired. He gestured widely in front of him, to the brownish-red boulders standing tall like fallen pieces of a distant planet in the middle of the desert.

'I thank you, fine lady, for accompanying me to the Casibari Rock Formations.'

He helped her unbuckle her helmet and held it as she shook out her hair. The sky was a deep blue, the scalding sun was trying its best to break through his sunscreen, and all around them cactuses sprang like gnarly hands from the dusty ground.

They'd left Esme playing on the beach with Jess and some other kids, and he'd seized his chance to get Sara alone— finally.

'They're so smooth and weird-looking,' she said about the rocks, stepping forward along the dusty path.

He couldn't help but see her bikini bottoms through her sarong; the curve of her ass. 'How did they get here?'

'No one really knows,' he said. Some people think aliens brought them here.'

She smiled. '"ET phone home"?' Her fuchsia sarong was billowing softly around her in the breeze. God, she was so beautiful. He could tell she didn't really know it. He wondered if there had been anyone serious in her life, since Esme's dad, and felt a sharp twinge of jealousy.

Sprinting onto a nearby rock ahead of her, he held a hand down. On the top of the huge, flat boulder, he watched Sara's face as she looked at Aruba, stretching out beneath their feet. They were about three kilometres from the capital, Oranjestad, where the ship was docked.

'On a clear day you can see Venezuela from here,' he told her, taking in the dusty browns, and then the emerald-greens and clear blues of the waters beyond. 'The first inhabitants from the Arawak tribe used to climb on these boulders and watch for storms on the eastern horizon.'

Sara lifted her sunglasses to her head and looked at him. 'You always did absorb this kind of stuff like a sponge. No wonder you took this job.'

He smiled, ran his eyes over her lips. 'How long did you say you've been doing these cruises?'

'This is only my second.'

He brushed a strand of hair from her face, gently. It coiled around his fingers. She didn't move, but she averted her gaze. Did he make her uncomfortable out here? Memories were funny things. He wanted to say he remembered the curves of her body, the way she'd used to moan when he pressed kisses on her ticklish tummy. But she'd made it quite clear that she wanted things to stay professional between them. He had to respect that.

'I know you love to see the world, but I still don't get why you're here—working, I mean.'

Sara lowered herself onto the rock and he did the same. She hugged her sarong-wrapped knees to her chest.

'You were pretty married to your family's practice, from what I recall.'

He was quiet for a moment and the birds sang in the silence.

'My father died two years ago,' he told her, watching a warbler flit from a tall bush. 'I put a locum in—just to get away for a while, you know? I did the cruise and really enjoyed it, and they asked me back for a second this year.'

'I'm so sorry.' Sara put a hand to his on top of his raised knee. Her voice was tight. 'About your dad. Fraser, I didn't know.'

'It was a heart attack.'

He missed his father, of course—he'd grown up worshipping the guy—but he'd never come to terms with the fact that his dad had resented his and Sara's relationship six years ago. Dr Philip Breckenridge had been an excellent doctor, but managing the finances of the practice had never been his strong point.

The money Fraser's late grandfather had left in trust for him was to have been released to him when Fraser qualified, on the proviso that he spent it to further his career. By pumping it back into the practice, Fraser would appease the practice trustees and save his parents from an uncertain retirement.

But when he'd gone to tell Sara he needed some time to concentrate on qualifying, so the money for the practice could be released, even knowing it wasn't great timing because her mother had just died, she'd already made her mind up.

'We should just call it a day, Fraser. It's too crazy right now; everything is changing.'

Her movement beside him startled him back to the present. Sara had turned to face him, cross-legged on the rock.

'I mean it, you know; I really *am* sorry about your dad, Fraser.'

'Thank you.'

'I know what it's like to lose a parent.' She curled her fingers around his, holding both his hands in the space between them.

His mind flashed back to them walking hand in hand around Edinburgh Castle, taking photos of each other on the cannons. She'd known grief herself then, of course, and he'd wanted to keep on helping her through it. He'd wanted her with or without all the problems surrounding them at the time.

But when he'd gone to London to see her, shortly afterwards, to tell her that he missed her and ask if they could figure things out somehow, he'd seen her with that…that guy.

'So, you live at home with your dad?' he asked her now. 'Because of Esme?'

He dropped her hands, took a bottle of water from his pack and took a swig, then splashed some against his face and chest.

'That's one of the reasons,' she said.

He noticed her eyes giving his abs an appreciative glance through his open shirt. He handed her the water.

'Haven't you ever moved in with a boyfriend, or…fiancé or anything? What about Esme's father? I saw you with him once, you know.'

Sara's eyes grew wide. She paused with her lips to the bottle and he realised he probably shouldn't have admitted it.

'You saw us?' she said. 'When?'

He shrugged. 'I'm assuming it was him. I came to see you in London a couple of weeks after you left. You'd already made it obvious you wanted to move on, but I guess I thought I could change your mind. I saw you with him outside that restaurant in your street…'

'You really did that? Came to London to see me?' She looked grief-stricken all over again for a moment. 'I can't believe you did that.'

He could see he'd upset her, but he had to ask. 'Would it have made a difference? If you'd seen me?'

She was quiet. 'I don't know. That was the one and only time we met, Fraser. We spent one night together and then he left the country for a job without ever knowing I got pregnant. It was a stupid thing to do, but I was still grieving for mum, and missing you, and for once in my life I'd had way too much to drink...'

'You don't have to explain.'

'So Esme wasn't exactly planned—not that I have any regrets.'

'Of course not. She's incredible, Sara.'

'She really is. I never knew I could love another human so much after...'

She trailed off, but he knew what she was going to say. After *him*. He'd never understood why she'd felt compelled to cut him out of her life so completely.

'Living with my dad seemed like the best way to care for him *and* Esme,' she continued. 'My grandparents lived in that house for over sixty years before they died. Did I ever tell you how the ceiling is peppered with marks from popped champagne corks? Over the years it's become a sort of map of my family's celebrations.'

'That's beautiful.'

He meant it. He'd been raised in a pristine house, where a champagne mark on a ceiling would have meant arguments, shouting, and a week of interior decorating right after.

Sara cast her eyes to the butterflies, swirling around another bush. 'I suppose I keep on hoping that one day soon we can pop another champagne cork to mark Esme's new kidney, and another for her sixteenth birthday, and one more for her wedding.' She let out a disgruntled sound. 'I just can't think of ever celebrating anything again until that first one happens. Sorry—I know that's weird.'

'It's not weird at all.'

Fraser kept his eyes on the ocean. To hell with the pain this woman was still going through, and the way it took the light from her eyes. It made her doubt herself and everything she did.

He took her face in his palms and she drew her hands over his impulsively. 'It *will* happen. We'll find a donor for Esme,' he told her resolutely.

'Help! Oh, my God, please help—is anyone there?'

The anguish in the voice caused them both to scramble up.

'Help!' The female voice came again. 'Over here!'

Springing into action, Fraser grabbed his bag and scrambled down the rocks with Sara, making sure she didn't slip. They raced further down the trail towards the sound until they found themselves face to face with a sight Fraser had never seen before.

Marcus, the kid in the green board shorts. who'd been mean to Esme on the beach, was lying on his stomach on the dusty ground. He was writhing around in pain with half a damn cactus sticking out of his backside.

Sara hurried to unfold a towel from their pack, so they could move him away from the dirt.

'He fell on it—he was running too fast!' his mother cried. Can you pull it out of him, Doctor? Should I?'

Fraser clasped her wrist. 'No, don't touch it!'

The woman in short blue dungarees and that giant sun hat was crouching over her son on the ground now, trying to hold him steady. 'It's not poisonous, is it?'

'It's not poisonous,' Fraser told her, spotting some fabric from Marcus's board shorts impaled on the offending cactus, just metres from two abandoned bicycles. 'Just try not to move,' he told the lad. 'We don't want these little suckers going any deeper—and don't put your hands near your mouth if you've touched the cactus at all, OK?'

'OK…' Marcus was sobbing. 'It hurts!'

'I know it does.' Sara's voice was soothing as she took tweezers from a small case. 'Luckily it looks like the glochids are mostly in one area, so just keep still like Dr Fraser said.'

Fraser readied the gauze and antiseptic as Sara went to work on Marcus's poor inflamed skin. His backside was so swollen it resembled a bright red beach ball. It was very lucky they'd been so close.

Back on the *Ocean Dream*, they whisked a sore Marcus to the medical centre. He and his mother were both adamant that they didn't want to leave the cruise, and Fraser tried to make them laugh by telling them all the things Marcus could still do standing up—like fishing, or tennis, or painting standing at an easel.

'You can also help me make my video, if you like,' Esme interrupted from the doorway, just as Fraser was handing Marcus's mother a prescription for painkillers. The kid now had a significant amount of gauze taped to his behind.

Marcus's cheeks flamed almost as red as his backside when he saw her.

'Esme, why are you here?' Sara walked over to her quickly. 'Where's Jess?'

'In there,' Esme said, pointing to the coffee house next door. In her long denim shorts and star-patterned shirt she walked past Sara and pointed at Marcus. 'What happened to you?'

Marcus wrinkled his nose. 'I fell on a cactus.'

Esme's little brow furrowed as she took in all the gauze. For a second Fraser thought she might laugh, or say something mean. Marcus had been mean to *her*, after all.

'That must have hurt,' she said instead, her eyes narrowed in concern. 'Are you OK?'

'I'm OK.' Marcus sniffed. 'Sorry I called you an alien.'

Esme grinned. 'I suppose I *do* look a bit like an alien sometimes. Do you want me to show you my robo-kidney when you're better?'

Fraser stood next to Sara as Esme explained how she needed the dialysis machine for her kidney to function. He could practically feel Sara swelling with pride as Esme offered to play with Marcus, so he wouldn't feel like the only funny-looking one on the ship.

'She's as compassionate as someone else I know,' he whispered to her, nudging her arm. Sara looked up at him.

'If only that was enough to make us a match.'

He felt his chest tighten. 'I told you, Cohen,' he said firmly. 'It's going to happen.'

CHAPTER FIVE

SARA TAPPED HER toes to the music as she relaxed against her headboard, keeping one ear out for the radio. *Knit one, pearl one, knit one, pearl one*, she mouthed, feeling herself sink into her project as though it were some kind of meditation.

A meditation on Fraser.

She'd been thinking about one of their first encounters. She'd agreed to do some tests on him, prior to a marathon he was running for charity—not the sexiest introduction, by anyone's standards, but he'd made it so. Maybe they both had. She'd seen him around St Enid's but he'd never talked to her before…never looked at her like that before.

Three nights later they'd been laughing over hospital politics in a posh Italian restaurant and she'd never been so smitten in her life.

'Are you in here?'

The voice behind the door made her heart lurch. He had a knack of showing up whenever she was thinking about him…which probably wasn't surprising, considering he'd been on her mind since the second she'd seen him again.

She shoved her knitting under the pillow. She had a sneaking suspicion Fraser had thought she was a geek, always glued to her needles like some kind of grandma. Smoothing down her ankle-length baby blue dress, she opened the door.

'Hey,' she said. 'You found me.'

'Looks like I did.' His handsome face looked even more tanned after their time outside at the beach. 'What are you doing?'

'Nothing.'

'Are you OK?'

'I'm OK.'

She was grateful for his attention, of course, though the slow burn of a fire that should have died a long time ago still made her weak and nervous. His blue eyes were searching. He'd sensed the thin ice she was standing on with Esme—the fear that came with never knowing when or if it would break—and his compassion was switching on that *thing* again inside her. He'd vowed to help, and he certainly knew a lot of important people. His family knew a lot of people. The more people on her team the better.

'I thought you'd be up on deck,' he said.

'Why?' She trailed her eyes along his triceps as he brought a hand up to rest it on the doorframe. His muscles flexed beneath his snug blue shirt. He was wearing khaki cargo shorts down to his knees, revealing toned and shapely calves.

'The tribute band?' he reminded her. 'They just did a pretty good job of Adele. I thought I'd come look for *"someone like you"*.'

She groaned at his pun, even before he started singing the song. He'd always sung in the shower. Sometimes she'd joined in.

'Come up and listen,' he cajoled. 'You've been working so much, and you shouldn't be cooped up in here alone.'

'I like the quiet,' she insisted, but his big hand on the doorway was moving towards her now, and seconds later he was pulling her out into the corridor, dancing with her down it towards the elevators as she laughed despite herself. Damn him.

The air up on deck was thick and muggy, hinting at a storm. It stuck to her skin like another layer of clothing as Fraser pulled out a chair at a table near the band. He slid her chair back in after she sat and offered to get her a drink.

'Let me guess—vodka and cranberry, minus the vodka?' His eyes were twinkling in the soft lights around the deck.

She was impressed. 'You remember.'

'I remember lots of things about you, Cohen. Wait right here.'

She watched his firm ass in his shorts as he made his way over to the bar; observed the way he walked, the way he turned heads wherever he went. He'd always been handsome, but over the last six years he'd grown even more so.

She'd insisted on staying professional and she had to stick to her guns—though she really, really wanted to run her hands over *his* guns. She groaned at her own thoughts.

When she turned back to the table Dr Renee Forster was heading towards her. She took the seat next to Sara.

'How's it going?' Renee crossed her long legs. 'You seem to be doing a great job with the dialysis patients. Did I see Dr Breckenridge playing with your daughter on the beach before?'

Sara cast her eyes to Fraser. He was still at the bar. 'Yes, they seem to have formed quite a connection.' She cleared her throat as she realised it was true. It was rare that Esme took to men as she'd taken to Fraser. She couldn't stop filming his 'funny faces' with her camera either.

'He's a good man,' Renee said. She placed a slim, manicured hand on top of Sara's and smiled. 'I always wondered who it was that stole his heart.'

She excused herself and sidled off again, just as Fraser placed a drink down in front of her and resumed his position on the chair.

'What did Renee want?'

'She told me you're a good man.'

'Well, she's got that right.'

Sara took a sip of her drink. He'd ordered the same. Fraser, as far as she knew, had always been teetotal. And she hadn't had a real drink in years—although right now she was pretty tempted to order one. Renee's words were nice enough, but how much did she know about her and Fraser? How much did anyone on this ship know about their past?

She'd been thinking about their conversation on the rocks, when he'd told her he had come to London. What might have happened if she'd seen him there? She would have crumbled. But nothing would have changed in the end.

Then again, maybe *everything* would have changed.

'Nurse Cohen?' She turned in her seat to find Marcus standing there.

'How are you doing now, buddy?' Fraser asked. His arm was draped along the back of her chair.

'I'm feeling better,' Marcus said shyly. 'My mum said I should ask Nurse Cohen for a dance.'

He was looking at the floor now. Fraser's hand had found the back of her neck through her hair and she struggled to keep her face straight. She couldn't move—couldn't let her head sink back into the familiar comfort of his palm.

'I'd love to dance,' she said quickly, getting to her feet.

She put her hands on Marcus's shoulders. His head reached her belly button, half a metre away. He started shuffling his feet awkwardly on the deck and somewhere on the periphery of her vision she saw his mother take a photo on her phone.

Sara's eyes found Fraser, still at the table. He was sitting in shadow but his gaze was as piercing as if it was in full sunlight. If he'd come to see her in London he must have been more devastated over her leaving him than she'd assumed. Considering he'd been about to break up with her anyway, *why* had he done it?

When the song came to an end she was about to excuse herself from Marcus when Fraser strode over purposefully. His shadow seemed to fill the deck for a moment, his corded muscles even more defined in the low light and the fitted fabric of his blue shirt.

The lazy notes of a saxophone curled around the soft chatter as Marcus stepped aside.

'I was getting jealous over there,' he whispered into her ear, drawing her close.

She held her breath. The stars were twinkling above them. She'd never seen so many stars.

Her head came up to his chin, clean-shaven now. As he placed his hands on her waist she breathed in invisible clouds of his aftershave and that other scent, the one that was only Fraser... And with it came the memories—rolling in the bed, tumbling to the floor, laughing hysterically, then re-connecting, their backs being scratched by the carpet, the sheets over their heads.

He drew her close. 'I know how much you love this song,' he said, and she realised he was laughing softly.

They were playing *their* song—a slow, more provocative version of *Never Gonna Give You Up*.

She pressed her hands to his chest, laughing into his shirt. 'You asked them to play this?'

'Just for old times' sake. You smell incredible, by the way.' His fingers trailed slowly down the open back of her dress, leaving tingles in their wake.

'I was thinking the same about you.'

They started to dance. She pictured his shoes moving carefully around hers and wondered if they would ever find their feet together again. Her mind kept slipping from the strange here and now to his bedroom back then, at the start of it all.

The day they'd taken that undignified tumble from the bed to the carpet when they'd been listening to this song. They'd been cracking up at the fact that it had turned their sensual lovemaking into an instant eighties disco.

Her arms were circling his shoulders now. They were one night away from Grenada, and she couldn't wait to feel the sand there beneath her toes; beneath her back, as she made love to Fraser—maybe just once, *for old times' sake*.

She pulled away slightly. What was she *doing*?

'What were you knitting, back in your cabin?'

She could hear the smile lurking in his deep Scottish accent. His fingers had hardened at her retraction, refusing to let her get too far away.

'How do you know I was knitting?'

'I could hear the *click, click, click* through the door. I found it strangely arousing.'

Sara buried her face in his shoulder for a second as he repeated the clicking sound with his tongue.

'I used to imagine you sitting there knitting things for our kids. They'd either be too big or too small, and we'd have all these teddy bears and toys all over the house, all wearing your tiny knitted socks.'

'What would we do with the bigger ones?' she dared to ask him, though she wanted to ask when exactly he'd decided they'd have kids together one day.

'I'd save them for cold days...for protection,' he said into her ear.

'Is that right?'

His hair brushed her face softly as they danced, and she caught herself pressing closer against him, heart to heart, breathing in the steadying presence she'd missed and letting it claim her completely in the moment. God, they had been so good together—seriously good. They'd just...fitted.

She smiled against him as he moved with her to the music, but her thoughts refused to untangle.

She couldn't have Fraser *and* Esme. She had to focus on finding Esme a donor. Fraser was going home at some point anyway—back to Edinburgh, back to the life his father had planned for him from the start.

'She's no good for you, son. You're in danger of screwing it all up. What about your career? What about everything you've worked so hard for?'

His father's voice had been concerned, full of foreboding. It had made her shiver in her hidden place on the stairs. She'd saved Fraser the trouble of breaking it off—she'd barely waited till bedtime to get in there first. Pity the fool who came between members of the Breckenridge family, she'd thought.

It still stung that his father had been so unsympathetic, so cold as to try and drive them apart. It stung even more that Fraser had let her go without a fight. But what hurt the most now was knowing that he'd come to get her in London and she hadn't even known. Now their lives really were on different paths—more different than ever before.

Fraser's hands were on her waist still, controlling her closeness, even though the song had ended and the band were stepping off the stage. With every ounce of strength she possessed she forced herself to take a step back. The moon and the lights made a silhouette of his face. The spell was broken.

'What are we doing here, Fraser?'

He narrowed his eyes, but his reply was cut short by Harry, their cardiac patient, spinning through the crowd right up to their toes in his wheelchair.

'I've been looking for you!'

His bald head was gleaming pink under the disco ball, his puffy cheeks full of colour again. He'd made an excellent recovery. He motioned for Sara's hand and she watched in shock as he placed a giant wad of rolled-up bills into her palm and folded her fist over it.

'For you,' he said. 'My winnings from the casino that night.'

She shook her head quickly. 'I couldn't—'

'Plenty more where that came from. If it wasn't for you I wouldn't be here to spend it. So spend that, Nurse Cohen.' He released her and turned to Fraser. 'It's for both of you. Heaven-sent, both of you. And a match made *in* heaven, by the looks of it.'

CHAPTER SIX

'SHE'S FALLEN!'

Fraser heard the voice before he saw the elderly lady on the floor. She was sprawled in a pool of what looked like water, but might possibly be gin. He spotted a lime slice not too far away.

'Enid! Can you get up?'

A short man in a loud Hawaiian print shirt was fussing around her. Fraser moved him aside gently and reached for his radio. In what seemed like seconds his ears picked up the tapping of shoes on the deck.

'Stand back please,' came Sara's authoritative voice.

She appeared beside him with the stretcher as the crowds parted. He noticed several phones pointed at them.

'No filming, please,' she told them strictly, swiping a tendril of loose hair behind her ear. 'What happened?'

She was dressed in her white coat and fresh from the dialysis centre, he gathered. Her air of determination and swift efficiency, plus the lingering smell of her shampoo in the warm sea air, threw him right back to that summer with her in Scotland.

Enid was in her late seventies, maybe older. Her hair was pure white. 'She's having trouble moving,' he told Sara as she quickly handed him oxygen.

'Can you lift your leg, or turn it?'

Her voice was low, kind. He watched her hand move gently over Enid's hip and leg, inspecting for damage.

'Can you put any weight on this side?' Enid howled again.

Sara pulled a face and apologised. 'We have some swelling,' she announced.

He placed the oxygen mask over Enid's mouth.

'Looks like a break in the hip.'

She caught his eyes as she said it and he nodded, keeping his face expressionless so as not to panic Enid, or her Hawaiian-shirt-wearing husband. It was exactly as he'd feared.

'Will she be OK?' Mr Hawaiian Shirt looked panicked anyway. He sported one or two strands of white hair on an otherwise shiny head.

Fraser helped Sara lift Enid onto a stretcher. 'Are you her husband?'

'Yes, but we don't have insurance.' The man's face looked as white as his hair now.

'We'll do all we can. Come with us.'

'Should we call the Coast Guard?' Sara looked concerned. Enid was sucking in short, sharp breaths.

He shook his head. 'Not yet. I don't think we need to.'

She took the other end of the stretcher without so much as a flinch and together they lifted their patient and moved as one towards the top-deck entrance.

Now that they were inside, away from the eyes and phones and ears on deck, the old man asked him. 'How much will medevac cost?'

'Sir,' Fraser said, trying to keep his inner frown from showing in his face and voice. 'It's never good to travel without insurance. but that's not the main concern here. The main concern is your wife. We need a radiological diagnosis before—'

'What's that?' The guy looked flustered and confused. He started to sweat through his shirt as they headed for the elevator.

'X-rays,' Sara clarified, moving swiftly along.

Fraser was walking backwards now in the narrow walkway, and she was walking forward. He watched the sunlight from the porthole windows play in her hair the whole way.

'We'll take some X-rays and then we'll know more. Don't worry—we have it under control.'

She pushed the button for the elevator. Her hair was half pulled back in a bun and he noted her earrings suddenly— tiny little blue sapphire studs. She'd been driving him crazy all night, even after she'd gone to bed.

He'd thought about kissing her on the dance floor. God, he'd wanted to—or just nibble lightly on her ear for half a second. That had used to drive her wild. Holding her against him like that after all these years had made him think entirely unprofessional thoughts, but somehow he'd reined them in.

In the medical centre, they moved Enid off the stretcher and carefully onto a bed. Sara rolled the vitals machine over quickly while Fraser snipped with precision along the lady's floral skirt. He always felt bad cutting people's clothes.

The wheels of the X-ray machine screeched for a second on the shiny floor as Sara wheeled it over and plugged it in.

'Pulse is one hundred; blood pressure is eighty over fifty-five,' she told him.

Enid's husband loitered, watching, fanning himself with his own shirt. The room was hot, even under the whirring ceiling fans.

Fraser beckoned Sara to the corner of the room with him. 'We're almost at Grenada,' he said. The loose tendrils of her hair tickled his face under the fans as he leaned close. 'She's OK, but she'll be better off staying stable with us till we get to the island.'

'If you say so, Chief.'

He liked that word coming from her lips. 'I do.'

He cast an eye to Enid and her husband. He still couldn't believe some people travelled without insurance.

'Calling for medevac now will wind up costing them more

than waiting it out for an ambulance. And it won't make a difference to our Enid at this point. Get her some morphine.'

She turned to do exactly that. It still felt kind of mad that they were working together. He knew she was right to be wary—not just of him, now that he was practically a stranger again, but because so many staff relationships ended badly. Bad vibes between fighting colleagues made life awkward for everyone, and he knew Sara would never risk that around Esme.

'How long to Grenada?' she asked him.

'About one hour.'

Sara prepped the needle for the morphine—just a little… just enough to keep Enid out of pain. He watched her squeeze her hand reassuringly before administering it.

'We'll get her to a hospital on Grenada,' he said to Enid's husband. 'She'll be far more comfortable this way.'

The hour rolled by. Fraser made a call shore-side, transferred the X-rays, and had it confirmed by staff in Grenada that, yes, it was indeed a broken hip. Sara arranged for an ambulance at the port.

No one confirmed it had been spilt gin that had made Enid slip, but no one confirmed it had been water either.

'Is everything under control?'

Renee appeared after a brief knock at the door that gave them no time to move apart without her seeing them. He stepped away from Sara anyway. She did the same thing.

'Vitals are stable. The ambulance is headed for the port,' he told her, while Sara buried her head in her clipboard.

St George's Grenada was as busy as ever, but the crowds parted as he and Sara carried Enid off the ship and let the ambulance take her away.

'She'll be OK,' he said, watching it move along the road to the hospital, where he knew she'd be taken care of.

'She won't be getting back on the cruise, though, will she?' Sara sighed beside him. 'Should we not go to the hospital too?'

'She'll be going straight in for surgery, and she's in good hands. Also, she was probably having the best time of her life right before this,' he told her.

He spotted Renee again, talking to another passenger wearing a giant sunhat. Also distracting him now was a youngish looking couple, possibly in their late twenties, deep in some kind of chilling disagreement. The guy, sporting a long black ponytail and a bare back full of tattoos, was yelling in what looked like a drunken rage at a woman in a leopard-print dress. In turn, she was simmering, arms folded. Her body language screamed discomfort.

Fraser had seen them around the ship. They were always either smooching in a corner or arguing. *Bad vibes.*

He was about to walk over himself when two security guards stepped in. He put his hand on Sara's. 'Let's go somewhere else,' he said quickly.

'What's going on with them?'

'I don't know, but they don't look happy.'

He started unbuttoning his white coat, zipped it into his bag, and motioned her to follow him fast, before Renee or anyone else saw.

'Come on, Esme's safe with Jess—aren't you hungry for a taste of Grenada? We won't be long.'

'I *am* pretty hungry, now that you mention it.'

Sara followed him, taking off her own white coat quickly. He folded it into the bag with his as they walked, grateful that he'd worn jeans and a loose white shirt underneath.

Before long they were seated at his favourite restaurant. The ocean glistened in the distance and Sara looked relaxed, finally. He watched her blue sapphire studs reflecting the sun as she studied the scenery.

'So, drama aside, what can you tell me about this place that doesn't involve medical emergencies and ambulances, Mr Chief Tour Guide?' She picked up her cranberry juice.

He leaned back in his seat. 'Well, Grenada was founded

by the French in the early eighteenth century. That's why it looks so…'

'French?' She smiled as he rocked for a moment on his chair legs.

'Exactly.'

Vibrant red roof tiles on a patchwork of pastel-coloured houses stretched before them, right up to the ocean. Fraser thought Sara had never looked as pretty as she did in a setting like this. Six years on and he swore she was even more beautiful. Her eyes were wiser, though, as if she'd seen too much—as if she was stuck inside her own head at times, maybe missing something wonderful while processing bigger things. She was used to putting Esme first, of course.

'I'm guessing you don't go on holiday much?' he said as two plates of jerk chicken were placed before them.

'It's just hard with Esme. And with the hospital. They're understaffed as it is.'

'Megan is happy to help, though, and your dad?' He remembered her younger sister, Megan.

She picked up a fork. 'Yes, but it's not fair to keep asking them, really, and I always panic if I leave her anyway. This is the first time we've been able to come away with dialysis care.' She paused. 'I did go to Mexico with my sister once. It was…interesting.'

'Oh, yes?'

'Long story—some guy called Pedro.'

He fought a stab of jealousy. 'You hooked up with a guy called *Pedro*?'

She laughed. 'No, not me—Megan. I read books. That's my idea of a good time these days, Fraser. Books and knitting.'

'And the butterfly collection?'

She smiled. She'd always collected things with butterflies on them. He'd given her a butterfly-patterned lace bra once.

'You never felt the need to be the last to leave a party, but you could still start one whenever you wanted.' He lowered his voice, directed it across the table. 'Especially in the bedroom.' He couldn't resist. They both knew their sex-life had been incredible.

'Your father had so many plans for you,' she said after a moment, her lips still curved, smiling at the memories no doubt. 'He'd be proud of what you've done and what you're doing, Fraser.'

He reached across the table for her hand and she dropped her fork. 'I listened to him way too much.' He'd said it now.

'What do you mean?'

'He was always so set in his ways—you know that.'

His heart started to thrum. His father had been looming in the doorway after Sara had left in a taxi.

'She broke up with me. What did you say to her?'

'Nothing, son, I said nothing. But she's a smart girl—she knows she's bringing you down right now, Fraser. More to the point—wake up! There's more to life than women.'

'I know that.'

'Well, prove it, then. We need your help to keep this practice afloat. I know it's a lot to ask, son, but think of the future. Think of everything me and your mother have worked for. Now Sara's gone you'll have the space you need to get back on track!'

He'd had to bring Fraser's mother into it. God bless Aggie Breckenridge, who'd worked tirelessly her entire life to raise him, to keep the practice running, only to be told she might not be able to retire in the manner she deserved. They'd been ploughing every penny of their savings into modernising the practice and they'd still needed more.

He'd called and called Sara, determined to talk to her and tell her what he hadn't found the courage to admit before— that his family were under significant financial strain and needed him. He'd been determined that in spite of her concerns they could make it work.

But when he'd flown to London and seen her with someone else he'd accepted that maybe his father had been right.

He *had* been distracted from his studies. He'd had no other options then. He *couldn't* afford to let his family lose it all.

He'd kept his word, pulled himself up, got back on track. He'd qualified and then injected his trust fund money straight into the surgery, paying for new equipment, the latest treatments, three more highly qualified staff members. But he'd never forgotten Sara.

He stood and pulled her up from her seat, bringing both hands to her face.

'Fraser...'

His name was a breath as her hands came up again, over his. Their meals were forgotten.

'You and me, we had something really good,' he said, putting a hand to the back of her head and letting his fingers tangle in her soft hair as he touched his forehead to hers. 'We both know that.'

She closed her eyes.

'We were young,' he said. 'Maybe it just wasn't the right time for us back then.' He tilted her chin. 'When we get off the ship...'

'I don't know, Fraser.' She pulled away and her amber eyes seemed to rummage through his soul. 'Things are all so different. I can't do anything right now, with the way things are for Esme.'

'I know—and I know you're doing everything you can for Esme—but we're going to find her a donor.'

'You keep saying that...but how do you *know*?'

'I just do.'

He brought his nose to the tip of hers. He half expected her to pull away, or push him off, but her hands came to his chest. She clutched at the front of his shirt and he kissed her—because he had to.

Sara moaned slightly against his lips as she kissed him back softly, just for a second or two, before she pulled away and dipped her head against his shoulder. His arms circled her impulsively and they stood there, her hair brushing his face in the breeze, the scrape of forks on plates a distant sound.

He wanted to lead her off the terrace and do more. He wanted to take her back to the ship and make love to her. But for the moment this would have to do. This and working on the plan he'd been hatching. It was now taking on whole new proportions in his head...

CHAPTER SEVEN

SARA WOKE WITH a jolt and almost hit her head on the ceiling. She'd slept in a fit of crazy dreams featuring tsunamis and Fraser...maybe even surfing a tsunami with Fraser.

Someone was banging on her door.

'Sara!' Jess burst into her cabin, waving her spare key card. 'Sorry.'

She sprang up in bed, throwing the sheets off. 'What's wrong?'

'Esme's missing.'

She clocked the time. One-thirty a.m. 'Have you looked for her?'

'Yes, of course!'

She pulled on jeans and a T-shirt, and was instantly thrown back on the bed. There was a storm raging outside and the boat was rocking. Panic was a fire flaming on her skin, and then came chills at the thought of her vulnerable daughter, missing.

Jess put a hand to the wall to stop herself from tripping. 'I'm so sorry... I came in for my shift and she wasn't there—there was maybe a three-minute crossover between staff. She must have slipped out then, and I can't find her anywhere!'

On wobbly feet they climbed the stairs up to the nursery floor. Taking the elevator didn't feel right with the ship this unsteady. Outside the night was black. No stars. They were by now, en-route for Florida once more, but from the views outside they could have been anywhere.

'She can't have gone far,' Sara said, though her heart was

a sledgehammer. She felt more than queasy. The ground beneath her feet was unstable.

They checked the nursery again. She wasn't there.

'Where would she have gone?' Jess raked her hands through her hair. 'I'm so sorry, Sara. She knows she's not supposed to leave but she keeps on trying to do it.'

'You take the lower floors. I'll take the top. Tell Security on the way.'

Jess shot off in one direction and Sara took the stairs to the dining hall.

'Esme!' In the billiard hall she spun around. 'Esme!' The low lights were swaying on the ceiling, making shadows that slashed across the tables. She got down on her knees to check under the tables. 'Esme!'

Next came the aqua spa, then the hot tub room, where full-length windows revealed the ocean jumping above the covered well. No sign of Esme.

In an empty lounge with a shuttered bar she was starting to lose hope. She'd looked everywhere.

'Esme, where are you?'

The lights were off. An eerie chill cloaked her body.

'Sara? What are you doing out here?'

Turning around, she lost her balance and Fraser's hands shot to her forearms, holding her steady. He was clearly on duty and his white coat was open, revealing a red shirt.

'You're supposed to be in your cabin,' he said. His voice was gruff. 'It's too dangerous to be moving around in these conditions.'

'We've lost Esme.'

His eyebrows arched in concern. 'How long ago did she go missing?'

'About twenty minutes. We've looked everywhere. God, Fraser, what if she…?'

'She couldn't have got up on deck and fallen overboard. It's all locked up. She's inside somewhere.' Fraser pulled out his radio, calling Security as he stepped with her into the hallway again. 'Was she alone?'

He took her hand in a firm grip that kept her steady in more than one way. She'd been about to break. 'We think so, but we don't know for sure.'

Their surroundings creaked and dipped as they made their way down the halls. She told herself he knew the ship much better than she did—every part of it. He would find her.

The light in the third deck kitchen was on. Fraser stopped abruptly and her hands landed on the solid wall of his back as she stopped herself from falling.

'There shouldn't be anyone on kitchen duty at this time,' he told her, swiping his key card and taking her hand again.

The sight when the door slid open made Sara gasp. Esme was sitting on the floor with Marcus, between two huge steel cabinets. The wooden spoon in a giant tub of ice-cream between them spoke of her sins...and of what Sara knew could potentially harm her.

'Esme—no!' She ran and ducked for the spoon, then threw it heavily into the sink as if it was made of hot tar. Tears burned her eyes. 'What are you doing, running away in the middle of the night? You could have been hurt!'

'I'm sorry.'

They reached for each other at the same time. Esme's frightened face melted her heart in a second. Fear became relief and more tears that Sara had to swipe away.

Esme started to cry herself. Huge wails in Sara's ear as she hugged her in her arms. Marcus stood up guiltily, his cactus-prickled backside clearly no longer an issue.

'How did you get in here?' Fraser scooped up the tub of ice-cream and put it on the counter. He didn't slam it down but she knew he was angry. He'd been worried for Esme, too.

'We found a key card.' Marcus held it out to him. 'Esme wanted ice-cream.'

'She's not supposed to have ice-cream.' Sara turned to

her daughter's hot, wet face. 'Esme, you *know* you're not supposed to have ice-cream.'

Fraser was radioing someone—likely the kitchen staff. She felt his hand on her shoulder from behind, and exhaled deeply into Esme's hair.

'I only had two scoops.' She was sniffling now.

'It's OK.'

Fraser sent Marcus back to his cabin, being sure to take the key card from him first.

'We'll need to monitor her closely,' Sara told him, following him out into the corridor. Esme was a heavy weight in her tired arms.

'Let me take her,' he said, and he scooped her up as easily as he'd lifted the ice-cream.

She could see his concern for Esme etched on his face as deeply as hers as they made their way to the dialysis room—especially when Esme stopped him in the corridor.

'I feel sick,' she announced.

'I've got you, Spielberg.'

He started moving faster with her, running with one hand on the golden rail to keep them both steady as the ship rocked—less menacingly now, but still enough to topple him or upset Esme's stomach more. She could see her daughter's forehead was clammy. Esme *knew* she wasn't supposed to have ice-cream.

Fraser was trying to calm her. 'Wow, you've got heavier. Is that all the delicious dessert you just ate?'

Esme giggled in spite of her tears and again Sara felt so... grateful? In awe? Both. He was a natural with Esme.

In the dialysis room, she hurried for a bedpan as Fraser laid Esme down. She watched the way he acted, with such tenderness, and was thrown right back to their kiss on the terrace. It had shaken her. All the potential consequences and outcomes—those had been the tsunamis in her dreams.

'Do you still feel sick?' he was asking Esme now.

She nodded miserably.

'It's probably just seasickness and excitement,' Sara told him, stroking Esme's soft blonde hair. The little girl's eyes were red and swollen. 'She didn't eat that much. Two scoops, right, Esme?'

'Yes.'

Sara called Jess. Fraser prepared some insulin and shot her a look over the needle. He was asking if she was OK. She gave him a nod and his brow wrinkled under his hair.

'I'm OK.' Sara said it out loud. She was fine now, because Esme seemed fine, though she *knew* she shouldn't have eaten anything this late, or this near to her dialysis—least of all dairy.

Potassium levels increased whenever kidney function decreased, and things like ice-cream could cause all sorts of problems. She felt the guilt start to creep its way in. She shouldn't have brought her here, away from her usual daily routines, it was too risky.

Once Fraser had placed Esme carefully back in her bed in the nursery, he took Sara aside in the hallway. The last hour or so had passed in a blur and she was exhausted. She should probably go and sleep with Esme. But the way he was looking at her...

'You should stay with me,' he said.

She'd known he was going to say it.

'I'm just down the hall. It'll be even bumpier down on your level—you won't get any sleep.'

'I don't know if that's a good idea.'

Guilt was already making her want to run back to Esme, to cradle her in her arms, and now it was twice as strong because she also wanted to stay in Fraser's.

'I have a big enough space for two,' he said. He leaned in even closer, till his lips were almost brushing hers. 'And I really need to kiss you again. It's been too long.'

'It's been two days.' The scent of him filled the air in his suite as she stepped inside it behind him.

'So this is where they put you,' she said as her hand found the wall. Her heart bounced in her chest as the door closed.

'It's better when it's not moving.'

Her eyes rested on the four-poster bed as he walked to a huge couch smothered in cushions. Maybe she shouldn't feel guilty for being here. Things happened, and Esme was having an adventure she'd remember for the rest of her life. Maybe *she* was, too. Besides, they didn't have to sleep together. That would complicate things and she'd regret it tomorrow—she knew it.

She observed the mahogany backdrop of cupboards, shelves and wardrobes while he poured her a glass of water.

'There's a big storm coming in the next few days or so,' he said, handing it to her and guiding her onto the couch.

'I thought this *was* a storm.'

Fraser took off his white coat, draped it on the back of a tall leather armchair, then sat down next to her. 'This is nothing—just a prelude to the main event. We try to be in port when bad weather like this is predicted. How are you feeling?'

He was so close she could practically feel the sparks flying. 'I'm fine, thank you, Fraser. Really. And I appreciate what you did tonight.'

His hand covered hers completely, where he held it on her knee. 'I did what anyone would have done. But are you sure you're fine? You've had a bit of a scare.'

'I'm processing it. I'm glad you're here.'

He brought her hand to his lips and let them linger there a moment. She felt the familiar urge to be closer to him as tingles ran up her thighs.

'Esme's quite a handful, I can see,' he said, and she smiled, nodding.

He knew she'd been a mess, inside and out, probably, when Esme had gone missing. Did he also know the added torture of feeling so torn, like this? He was a total distraction from every moment she might have left with her daughter.

He took the empty glass from her. 'So...you can sleep in the bed and I'll take the couch.'

What? Sara blinked as he got to his feet. She hadn't been expecting that. She watched as he went about getting some blankets and a pillow from a cupboard above the bed and—forget the excuses—all she could think was, *No way...no way. How dare you do this to me now?*

So she said, 'Stop it, Fraser. You're not sleeping on the couch.'

She stood up, realising how forward she'd been but feigning confidence anyway. 'You've just worked a long shift. You should definitely have the bed.'

He dropped the spare blankets onto the quilt cover and raised his eyebrows. 'I am kind of tired. I guess if you insist...'

She watched him put his fingers to his shirt and pop the buttons one by one, slowly, on purpose, to make her smile. He unbuckled his jeans and she trailed her eyes over his lean, muscular thighs as he shook them aside. This was ridiculous.

'Having second thoughts?' he asked provocatively. 'You know it's much better when we stick together.'

He pulled the quilt aside, and when she reached him he pulled her close and kissed her in a way that made the bouncing in her chest turn to explosions. She raised her arms and he helped her off with her clothes, down to her underwear, stopping to admire her body just as he'd used to.

'I probably look different now,' she said, a little shy suddenly.

'Not so different,' he told her, stepping back to appraise her.

She saw the desire in his eyes and it boosted her, somehow. It had been a long time since anyone had seen her like this.

Still standing, Fraser swept her hair aside and kissed her neck, then her lips, and when the ship tilted they fell to the bed, still kissing. But when he pulled the sheets around them he spooned her from behind, holding her close.

'Much safer in here,' he whispered into the back of her neck. 'Remember the first time we slept together?'

He ran a hand along the length of her body, leaving flames in its wake. She wouldn't tell him she'd been thinking the same thing...or how much she was burning to have him touch more of her.

That first time they'd been in a bed smaller than anything on the cruise ship, in her student lodgings, drunk on each other...and she just a little on cheap Chardonnay.

'How could I forget?' she smiled. 'We broke a wine glass.'

'We're not doing that now, though,' he said, nuzzling her neck and lacing his fingers through hers.

'We don't have any wine glasses,' she whispered.

'That's not what I meant. We're not making love, because I know you'll wish you hadn't in the morning. Even though I want to do that with you all...night...long.'

She sucked in a breath. Her heart was a freight train. He knew her so well.

'Who says we would have slept together? The past is the past,' she said defensively.

But he chuckled and pulled her in tighter, and said nothing.

The rocking of the waves, now much gentler, lulled them to sleep eventually, and she dozed with her back to his chest and his arms locked around her. She had no dreams that she could remember; she just felt safe and content. But when sunrise crept through the windows she sat bolt upright.

The bed behind her was empty. Fraser was already gone.

CHAPTER EIGHT

THE SUN WAS hot on Fraser's shoulders as he swigged his coffee and crossed the street onto the Florida pavement. His mind was still racing over the details of last night, and the sight of Sara's head on his pillow after all this time.

It was a miracle they'd stopped at just kissing, but having her in his bed and in his arms again had filled him with fresh hope, and he was damned if he was going to ruin that by having her over-analyse any heat-of-the-moment sexual encounters—as he knew she would. Not unless the time was completely right.

She was worth waiting for.

The waiting room was empty when he walked in. He was more nervous than he'd anticipated he would be as he approached the young red-haired receptionist. The words *'Someone you know is hoping for someone like you,'* were framed on the wall behind her. He took it as a sign that he was doing the right thing.

'Fraser Breckenridge—good to see you again.' Boyd Phillips appeared from the hallway and offered his familiar firm handshake before motioning him through to a seat in a small quiet room.

'Thank you for seeing me at such short notice, buddy.' Fraser realised he was wringing his hands in his lap and moved them quickly to the arms of the chair.

Boyd noticed. 'Always happy to squeeze someone like you in. Everything OK? You look nervous.'

'I'm a little nervous,' he admitted, 'but only 'cause I might not be eligible.'

Boyd studied him over the rims of his glasses. 'Understandable. This is an admirable decision, and obviously an important one to you.'

A cactus sat between them, along with a photo of Boyd and his husband Bob, an addiction psychiatrist he'd met at a conference right here in Florida.

'I feel like it's the right decision,' he said.

'Aye, well, that feeling will help you a lot in the weeks to come. Hold on to that.'

'Yes, sir.'

Boyd gathered a set of forms that had to be filled out before proceeding with the tests. Fraser was grateful he actually knew this man, and could trust him. They'd known each other a long time, and Fraser knew Boyd probably wanted to ask him more than he was asking, but Boyd stuck to the essentials, as he'd hoped he would.

He knew the psychologist would be a different story.

Speaking to a psychologist was standard for non-directed kidney donors. And, in a green-carpeted room next to Boyd's, covered in posters much like the one in the waiting room, Fraser was made to talk about his reasons for wanting to donate.

The psychologist, a woman who looked considerably younger than Fraser's thirty-two years, was twizzling a pen in her manicured fingers, pursing her painted lips thoughtfully between questions.

'I used to be in a relationship with this little girl's mother.'

'Interesting... How long ago?'

'Six years, more or less. You could say life got in the way.'

'What do you mean?' She was drumming the pen on her knee now.

'Well, we were pretty young back then. I had to focus on my career and my family's practice in Edinburgh, while she moved back to London to help her family. Her mum died, and she had to… It's a long story. We just met up again.'

'How?'

'How did we meet up again?' He paused.

She was looking at him intently. He couldn't exactly tell her he'd done his best to ensure they were on the same cruise ship in spite of knowing Sara probably wouldn't have wanted to see him. He hoped things were different now.

'As I said before, we're both working on the *Ocean Dream*. I found out her daughter Esme is on dialysis. She's part of a new programme on the ship to care for the dialysis patients while they have a vacation. I suppose I saw things through both Esme's and her mother's eyes, and if I'm able to donate I want to.'

The psychologist chewed on her lip and scribbled on her clipboard, studying the forms Boyd had passed to her. She crossed one leg over the other and looked him in the eyes. 'Is it possible you're doing this just to get back into a relationship with this child's mother?'

Fraser sat back in his seat. He forced his gaze to stay directly on hers. The question shouldn't have surprised him at all. Obviously she wanted to know he was doing this for the right reasons. He couldn't deny it all came back to Sara. But, whatever happened between them in the future, this was still something he wanted to do. If Esme had been Sara's niece, or cousin, or even the daughter of a friend, having seen first-hand the struggle they were enduring, he'd have wanted to help if he could.

'I asked myself that at first,' he said, 'but, no. I'm a professional. I live to help those I can help—as do we all. I would do this for Esme whether Sara and I were together or not.'

'I see.'

He found himself smiling, picturing Esme's little face and enquiring eyes. 'You should see this kid—she's incredible. She has this camcorder that she takes everywhere. She's the brightest thing—always asking questions, making life out to be an adventure. I just want that to continue for her, you know?'

The woman started scribbling furiously, and although he was itching to find out what she was writing he shut his mouth. He had to let her make her assessment. He just prayed he'd said and done enough.

Next up was the urine test.

'This is the fun part,' Boyd said as his intern, a gangly guy with braces called Rishi, presented Fraser with a tube.

He was led down a sunlit corridor to the bathroom. Palm trees waved at him from outside through the windows. Sara would be awake now, probably wondering where he'd gone, and a twinge of guilt struck him. He hadn't told her his plan.

'As I'm sure you know, this test will throw into the light any sign of infection or other abnormalities,' Rishi told him. 'If we find any sort of blood, protein or glucose in your good stuff, Dr Breckenridge, you won't be able to donate. You've said you're not on any meds, any antibiotics…?'

'No, I'm not, that's correct,' he said.

'OK, then, we'll be right here when you're done.'

Fraser stepped into the bathroom. He knew he was fine already—he'd done his own tests prior to this. He'd been torturing himself by doing that, really, because whatever the tests told him didn't matter—the experts had to make their own minds up. It was Esme's health at stake… Esme's life.

He'd wanted to tell Sara what he was planning, of course, but at the same time knew it was probably too soon. He'd see if he was eligible to donate first, then he'd tell her. He'd asked Boyd about other options via email and on the phone, and he was on the case already, but what would be the point of getting her hopes up about *him* as a donor before he knew if he could help? They were there to enjoy Esme's first real holiday—not to wait on tenterhooks for something that might not happen.

Fraser's urine sample was placed into a container with some others as Boyd continued with his questions from behind his desk. He wondered exactly how many people were planning to donate right now, at this very minute. How many people had sat in this chair before him, willing to donate a part of themselves to help someone else?

'We'll be checking your blood for potentially harmful viruses. Things like hepatitis, HIV… Any nasty infection that could be passed to your intended donor will rule you out.'

Fraser didn't even flinch as the needle was inserted.

'We're also seeing how well your kidneys, liver and other organs are functioning… Your forms say you don't drink?'

'No, sir—I never have.'

'I remember that, actually.'

'I don't smoke, I don't drink—I also don't run marathons any more.'

Boyd flashed Fraser's pecs an appreciative smile. 'Doesn't look like you need to. The ship's gym seems to be doing you some favours.'

'Why, thank you.'

Boyd readied another needle. 'We're also making sure you have enough blood, and that your blood clots properly.'

'Understood.'

'This is just the start of quite a lengthy process, Fraser— I'm sure you know that.'

'I'm sure it'll be worth it.'

'I remember Sara,' Boyd responded, taking Fraser by surprise.

He was testing his glomerular filtration rate—GFR— which involved an injection of a chemical into a vein in his arm. Again, Fraser didn't flinch. The GFR test would measure his kidney's ability to clear the blood of the substance that had been injected.

'I remember you talking about her long after you broke things off.'

Fraser drummed his fingers on the chair's arm, watching the liquid empty from the syringe. Who had he been kidding, thinking Boyd wouldn't say something eventually?

Of *course* he'd talked about her—he'd loved her. He always had and everyone knew it. And to love Sara was to love everything about her—especially Esme.

CHAPTER NINE

'HER HEART-RATE SHOWS one hundred and three. It climbs when she moves so she's clearly still in pain, likely from the vomiting.' Fraser turned from Sara back to their sweaty young patient. 'Where does it still hurt?'

'Here,' the girl said, putting her hands to her stomach. 'I think I'm going to throw up again.'

Sara helped the teenage girl out of her vomit-covered T-shirt and into a clean white one. The teen appeared to have contracted some kind of respiratory infection, and Fraser had his suspicions as to what it was.

'Lucky you came to us when you did,' Sara said kindly. She was fetching another bedpan now, just in case. She didn't look up at him as she worked. She hadn't done all afternoon. He knew he was still in the doghouse.

'Take care of this please, Chief?' she said to him, again without making eye contact.

She handed him the dirty T-shirt. He took it, glad of his rubber gloves. Sara could have just thrown it into the laundry bin herself, but he said nothing. She was still mad at him for disappearing on her. She had every right to be; he'd left her lying alone in his bed, after all.

But she'd looked so peaceful there. And, God, he'd missed the sight of that face, still and silent, her hair splayed on his pillowcase.

'Were there any other women after me?' she'd asked him before they'd drifted off.

'A couple,' he'd admitted. 'But none that made me feel like this.'

'Like what?'

'Like we could all go down on this ship and I wouldn't care as long as I was holding you like this.'

The second he'd said it he'd regretted it, because Sara wouldn't think of him if that happened—she'd think of Esme. Esme would always come first... And if he'd tried to explain then where he was going at such an early hour she'd have wanted to come too.

Either that or she'd have stopped him going. He wasn't sure which.

The phone rang. Sara beat him to it. He watched her movements in her long white coat and too-white sneakers as she held the receiver to her ear. She was tanned already... she was glowing.

'We have the results,' she told him a few minutes later.

He walked closer, out of earshot of their patient. 'The urine antigen?'

'It's not Legionnaires'—it's Pontiac fever.' She finally met his eyes.

They could be at odds with each other as much as Sara Cohen wanted, he thought. It didn't change what had happened, or the fact that their closeness had dredged up some long-suppressed feelings. Sure, they'd just about managed to keep it platonic, but he knew they'd *both* been fighting doing more in his bed.

Fraser cleared his throat. 'OK,' he said, 'Pontiac we can deal with.'

Better than Legionnaires'.

He didn't say it out loud. He didn't need to. They were both thinking it. During his last cruise they'd had a case of that, and the ship had been forced to cordon off the hot tubs. It was rare in people under fifty, but not unheard of.

'Have you been in the hot tub or the swimming pool in

the last few days?' he asked the teen. Her long red hair was stringy with sweat.

'No. Can I go now?'

'No.'

She started coughing again wildly, into her hand. Her forehead was glistening with sweat.

'You're not going anywhere,' Sara told her pointedly. Fraser watched her put a hand to her back and pat her gently. 'Sorry to say, but it looks like you have something called Pontiac fever.'

'What's that?' She looked horrified, her red hair sticking to her pallid face.

Fraser let Sara explain while he fixed an IV and its tubes.

'It's a milder form of Legionnaire's Disease…'

'A *disease*?' She looked even more horrified now.

'It's not transmitted from person to person, but it *is* contracted by inhaling bad bacteria from water. Did you sit under any kind of water jet or spray anywhere? Go anywhere with strange air-conditioning?'

The girl wrinkled her nose. 'No, I don't think so.'

'Think,' Fraser told her. 'It's important.'

'She *is* thinking, Fr… Doctor.' Sara paused. 'She's battling a fever. It's OK if you can't remember, honey.'

That had told *him*. He frowned in her direction and she pretended not to see. She'd said it in such a way that only he would know how annoyed she was—at *him*, obviously, not at the girl for her understandably cloudy memory.

He let it go. She was stressed about a Legionnaires' outbreak. She was thinking of Esme and the other dialysis patients. Those with weak immune systems were more likely to contract the condition, which put the dialysis patients at high risk should there be an issue with the ship.

He adjusted the IV as the teen swiped at her clammy face with a cool towel. 'Actually, there were ventilators pointed at us in that seafood restaurant.'

'Which restaurant?' Sara's voice was calm but anxiety was practically a cloud around her.

'Back in Florida. I knew that place was dodgy. Mum said it had the best prawns, but she really meant the cheapest. We won this cruise in a competition, you know?'

'Where's your mother now?' he asked.

'I don't know. She doesn't know I'm here.'

Fraser looked at Sara. They spoke without words. They had to find this girl's mother as soon as possible for tests. Even if she wasn't showing any symptoms it was better to be safe than sorry. Both Legionnaires' and Pontiac could take a couple of weeks to manifest at times, though it was deeply unlucky to contract either.

Sara ushered him aside while the teen hacked some more behind them.

'I'll call Miami. Tell them to report this—see if it links to any other clusters of Pontiac. There haven't been any other cases on the *Ocean Dream*?'

'Not yet on this trip. Never on any trip before, and not on this ship. It's practically brand-new.'

'Are you sure?'

She searched his eyes. He wanted to touch her.

'I'm sure. Cohen, I know what you're thinking, but it's probably a one-off. It's not contagious.'

'I know, but what if something has been overlooked?'

'Highly unlikely—they've triple-tested everything on here.' He couldn't help it. He placed his hands firmly on her shoulders. 'Sara, they wouldn't have allowed dialysis patients on board at all if there was any doubt that it was safe. You *know* this.'

She bit her lip. He'd never seen her so riled up in a medical setting. Keeping her status as a mother separate from that of a nurse must be tough in times like this. He pictured Boyd back at the clinic, running the tests, concluding...hopefully any day now...that he could be a donor for Esme.

'You're probably right,' she said, drumming her fingers on her leg.

Her hair brushed his fingers.

'I know you're right. It was the restaurant.'

'I'm sure it was the restaurant. We'll call them right now.'

CHAPTER TEN

SARA TRIED TO ignore the way her knee kept nudging Fraser's unbidden in the back of the buggy.

'This is one of my favourite islands,' he said as they started the bumpy, winding journey away from the bustling port where they'd docked in the Bahamas.

Esme looked wonderstruck, sitting on his knee, taking it all in. She had wanted Fraser to come with them to the pineapple plantation, the same way she'd wanted him at the beach in Aruba that time, and most evenings at their dinner table.

Sara's brow creased involuntarily under her sun hat as she fanned herself with a map. She couldn't exactly have argued with her daughter. They had been instructed to leave the ship anyway.

Renee had promised to call as soon as she'd heard from the seafood restaurant and had the ship's engineers check everything out again, just to be sure the problem didn't lie there.

She wasn't proud of the way she'd cracked over the Pontiac fever case. The times when Esme's health might be further at risk were the only times that it interfered with her job. The thought of what might happen to Esme or any of the other dialysis patients should there be any trace of Pontiac on the ship was not even worth contemplating. At least Fraser understood that.

He was filming Esme now. She listened as the little girl gave him a running commentary on the types of trees they were passing. She was making up names for them all.

'Mummy, Mummy, look—that's the Sara tree, and that's the Dr Fraser tree!'

'That's great,' she replied as Fraser cheered. She was trying and probably failing to sound upbeat. Esme always knew when she was down. She was usually the one to bring her up.

Esme looked enchanted now, though. Fraser seemed to love telling her stories about the time he went travelling. Before they'd met, and before his medical studies began, he'd spent six months seeing South America—the Galapagos, Ecuador, Chile and Peru. He was feeding Esme's imagination at every opportunity, answering her endless questions, and it unsettled Sara more than she could say, because she knew Esme dreamed of having a father figure in her life although Sara had always told herself they didn't need one.

'This is a very important part of the Bahamas, Esme,' Fraser was saying now in his best tour guide voice. 'The British settled here in the seventeen-hundreds—you can see it in the architecture. Looks a bit like home, don't you think?'

Esme wrinkled her nose.

'It doesn't look anything like the Britain *I* know,' Sara told him, smiling in spite of herself. It really didn't. It was a lot hotter, too. Her map was falling apart.

'You OK?' Fraser asked her, putting a hand to her knee suddenly. 'You're very quiet. I'm sure we'll hear something soon.'

'I hope so.' He squeezed her knee and she resisted the urge to touch him back. She was still annoyed with him for slipping out the other morning without waking her. He was hiding something—she could feel it.

When they reached the pineapple plantation she lingered behind, gathering her thoughts.

'They look like pine cones, Mummy!' Esme cried, pointing at the baby pineapples poking from their spiky green leaves on the ground.

She was filming everything, as usual. There were rows

and rows and rows of them, stretching into the distance under the grey sky.

'Come on, Cohen, you're falling behind! You don't want to miss out on planting your own pineapple, do you? We'll name it after you.'

Fraser stopped on the trail between the rows of plants. His black curls were sticking out around his red baseball cap. His eyes narrowed when she caught up to him.

'You're not still angry at me, are you? I told you—I had to go and see some people and it was too early to wake you up.'

'I'm not angry.'

'So you've been avoiding looking me in the eye for no reason, have you?'

Sara stopped in her tracks. She crossed her arms automatically, cutting him off like a roadblock. The slight breeze was picking up the bottom of her turquoise dress and trying to ruffle it against his khaki shorts, as if even their clothing couldn't keep away from each other.

'Fraser. I know you. I know you're keeping things from me.'

He stepped closer and stared into her sunglasses.

'I can't have men around who lie to me,' she continued, lifting the glasses up to her head so she could look him straight in the eye. 'Not with Esme. She's been through enough. *I've* been through enough.'

'I understand. It's nothing for you to worry about, I promise you.'

'Is it someone else?' She felt embarrassed the second he frowned.

'Is that what you really think? Cohen, I can barely even keep up with *you*.'

He looked genuinely offended at her words. She kicked herself internally as he looked away and out at the pineapples.

'I'm sorry,' she said, ramming a hand through her hair. 'It's just everything's getting a little overwhelming, you know? I told you we should focus on our work, I told you this couldn't happen, but I did it anyway.'

She went to walk past him but he caught her arm, drew her back. His eyes drilled into hers. She pulled her glasses back down to protect her thoughts.

'OK, so you're angry at yourself—I get it. But don't take it out on me and don't beat yourself up over something so stupid.' He lowered his voice. 'We didn't even *do* anything, Sara...'

'I should have been with Esme.'

'You were where you wanted to be,' he said. 'You were where *I* wanted you to be. And I'll tell you where I was the other morning, but not yet. Sara, you know me. You'll just have to trust me.'

A young girl no older than seventeen, in a flower-patterned headscarf, was explaining the pineapple industry in Eleuthera with pride, but all Sara could think about as she went along with the tour was Fraser, always two steps behind her, his eyes burning into her back like the sun.

She was being too hard on him.

It was easier being hard on him.

Their guide started leading them down another path towards an open patch of land. Three people were on their hands and knees in the dirt, planting baby plants and sowing seeds. Sara watched as Esme was led over to them and handed a seedling.

'Will you film me, Dr Fraser?'

'You bet I will.' He took the camera. 'Tell me what you're doing—don't miss anything out.'

Esme launched into a comical explanation as she went along, talking straight into the lens.

'He's so good with her,' the guide whispered at her side.

'He is—very good with her,' she agreed, noting how Fraser treated Esme like an equal, rather than a broken little kid. Esme adored him for it already.

'Cover it up with more dirt!'

Esme had buried the baby plant and was patting the dark soil firmly all around it to keep it in place. Everyone clapped and she beamed as if she'd just performed the greatest task on Earth.

'You should plant one too,' she announced. She picked up another seedling and held it out to Sara. 'Plant it with Dr Fraser, Mummy. You have to share it.'

Sara got on her knees beside him and he handed her a tiny shovel. Her fingers brushed his as she took it and she felt those sparks again, the need to hold her breath. She'd wanted nothing more than to make love with him, to reconnect the real way, but he'd been adamant they keep things PG-rated. Was it because he'd known he was about to get up early and leave, and not tell her where he was going?

'Is here OK?' Fraser asked Esme. 'You getting a good shot, Spielberg?'

'Here is perfect—plant it next to mine!'

Sara dug with the tiny shovel, trying not to over-analyse everything that was going on with Fraser. Instead she found herself studying Esme in the sunlight. The way her little nose and eyes crinkled as she concentrated was adorable. She'd long thought these quirks and expressions reminded her of something and had always assumed it was home. If home could be a person, not a place.

Their guide crouched down, smiling with kind eyes. 'You know, in two years' time you can come back and pick your fruit to eat.'

'I might not have two years,' Esme said bluntly, pointing to the line poking out above her clothing. 'See this catheter? It means I have a robo-kidney. They're really smart, but they don't keep you alive for ever.'

'Baby, don't say things like that!' Sara was horrified.

The poor guide looked frazzled.

'It's true, though, Mummy. Isn't it, Dr Fraser?'

Sara felt sick. She tried to stand but she felt Fraser taking her elbow, keeping her in place.

He turned to Esme. 'Of course you have two years—and much more than that, lass. You've got a whole lot of exciting stuff still to do.'

'But I don't have a donor.'

Esme sounded matter-of-fact, as if she'd thought about this endlessly and had come to terms with it. It made everything so much worse.

Sara let Fraser hold her down, trying to soak up his strength. He was right. She had to act normal. But this kind of thing *was* normal for her. Maybe it always would be.

CHAPTER ELEVEN

'ARE YOU READY to watch your mum do something really cool?'

Esme jumped up and down with glee as Fraser led them all to where an instructor was pulling lifejackets out of a plastic container on the shoreline, three feet away. Fraser took a small one and carefully buckled Esme into it. Sunbeams were glinting off his sun-kissed skin. He stepped closer to help Sara fasten the straps of her own lifejacket.

'No need to worry,' he told her, inches from her face. 'This guy knows what he's doing with newbies.'

The way he tugged on the straps was possessive, purposeful, pulling Sara closer to him with each tug.

'I trust him,' she said. She looked Fraser in the eyes. 'I trust *you*.'

He smiled, but cocked an eyebrow. 'Do you?'

'I want to.'

'I'll take that for now.'

He winked at her and she knew their earlier confrontation was forgotten. Of course she didn't think there was anyone else. He was hiding *something*, but he'd told her he would tell her eventually—which probably meant it was a surprise or something. She wouldn't put it past him; he'd always been a huge romantic.

At any rate, they had bigger concerns.

'Any word from Renee about the ship yet?' she asked him. Already she was hot in the lifejacket. The water was a pale inviting blue on the white sand.

He pulled out his phone for the hundredth time in the last hour and checked it. 'Nothing. I'm sure everything is under control. No news is good news, right?'

Sara frowned as he dropped it into a waterproof bag. That wasn't always the case. They'd had no news about a donor for Esme, *ever*.

She found herself resisting the urge to let her fingers rub a smear of sunscreen into his shoulder as he turned to their instructor, Ruben. How she'd let him talk her into going out on water skis she had no clue, but this was *her* holiday, too. She had to find something to tell her sister about—something exciting that she'd never done before.

'OK, you're looking good,' Fraser said, and she watched his gaze sweep her breasts in her bikini, and then her legs as he stepped back on the sand. 'You're looking *really* good. But I've told you that before.'

'Have you been water skiing before, either of you?' Ruben asked them. He was short and bald, in a black T-shirt and board shorts.

Sara shook her head, no, as Fraser said yes. She couldn't help her eyes lingering on the grooves of his six-pack as he pulled on his own lifejacket, recalling how she'd run her hands over him, her lips glued to his, almost desperate for more after so long apart.

She tried to focus as Ruben demonstrated how to make the most of her time on the water. 'Now, the important thing to remember is that if you fall, don't resist—just let go.'

'Don't resist—just let go. OK.'

They covered how she should assume the proper cannonball position, how she should keep her knees together, and how to let the boat do all the work—and the whole time Fraser nodded and murmured in agreement, as though he'd done it a thousand times and couldn't wait to get in the water.

She wondered whether anything ever scared Fraser Breckenridge, because if it did she'd never seen it. Except his father, she thought suddenly, surprising herself. And the thought of losing his mother. Fraser had always put his family first.

In the tender boat, Fraser made sure she and Esme were seated properly before he took his place beside her. Esme was beside herself with excitement. Sara watched her film Fraser putting a medi-bag into a waterproof bag.

'You're not about to miss a second, are you Spielberg?' Fraser laughed. 'How long is this movie going to be when you're done?'

'Long enough for two sequels,' Sara told him, shaking her head.

Before long they were chugging out into the turquoise water. Every now and then she caught the reflection of another boat or a snorkeler in Fraser's sunglasses as the scenery swept past.

'Do you want to go first, or should I?' he asked, breaking into her thoughts.

She turned to him. The wind was tugging his hair in all directions. She noticed a few flecks of grey in his stubble she'd never seen before.

'I think you should go first,' she said.

'That could be a bad idea.'

'Why?'

'What if you're so intimidated by how awesome I am that you don't even want to take your turn?'

She laughed. 'If anything, I'll be better than you. I don't weigh as much.'

He made a *pffft* sound. 'I don't think weight has anything to do with it.'

Their instructor turned around. 'Actually, the skis are made for different weight ranges, so it is quite important to use a pair that suits your size.'

Sara smirked. 'Better stick to medicine, Chief.'

'Fine, I'll go first. Show you how the pros do it.'

Ruben glided the boat to a stop and turned off the engine.

Fraser stood up, puffing out his chest in the lifejacket, making Esme giggle.

The boat was bobbing now that they were on relatively open water. A jet ski was already cutting through the waves nearby. The couple on the back were passengers on the *Ocean Dream*—the pair who were always arguing, Sara realised now, noting the guy's long ponytail and his back patterned with tattoos.

She turned to Fraser, now sliding his feet into the bindings.

'Ready!' he called, assuming the starting position.

The muscles rippled in his arms as he gripped the handle. He looked like some kind of James Bond extra, wearing black gloves and red shorts. He gave the camera a salute before Ruben drove on a little faster, then faster, till Fraser rose on the skis, standing up straight, skidding along behind them.

Sara watched in awe as his body twisted and weaved in the waves. The wind seemed to soften, allowing him to be at one with the water...right before he hit a rogue wave and toppled over.

Sara's breath caught. Fraser disappeared, but in seconds he was popping up again, straight back onto the skis, skidding on the surface as before. Esme was squealing in delight. The spray showered up around him in all directions. James Bond had nothing on Fraser.

Something else caught her eye. She froze. There in the surf to the right of Fraser, shining and glittering and leaping, was a dolphin.

'Esme, look!' she cried.

Esme's eyes grew round. Fraser had seen it too. He steadied himself expertly as the dolphin continued to swim alongside him. Mesmerised, Sara watched its long, silvery body gleaming in the light before it reached the boat and appeared to circle around them.

'Wow!'

The dolphin darted and zipped underneath the boat, and

then swam alongside, leaping and bounding in their spray. She turned to look for Fraser again, but what met her eyes was a scene of horror.

The couple on the jet-ski were heading straight for him. *'Fraser!'*

In a blink it was over. The rope was flailing on the water but Fraser had disappeared.?

'Fraser!' Hot tears flooded her eyes as she scrambled to try and see him. 'Where is he?' She turned to Ruben. 'He's gone!'

Esme was crying.

'It's OK, baby,' she soothed her.

Ruben cut the engine. The girl on the jet-ski was scream-ing hysterically. Mr Ponytail looked panicked. In a second Sara was in the water, swimming as fast as she could to-wards the spot where they'd collided. But swimming was not her strong point. A million scenarios screamed through her head, even as her professional voice was telling her to stay calm, to conserve her energy.

He still hadn't surfaced. Then there was a movement in the water below her. A hand on her leg. She drew in a sharp breath, spinning around. Fraser was coming up right in front of her, blinking. She reached for him, holding on to his life-jacket, letting them float along together while she caught her breath. Tears were still stinging her eyes with the salt water.

'I'm OK.'

She saw the panic in his eyes. His wet, handsome face was dripping an inch from hers.

'I'm OK. But the coral got me.'

She released him. 'What?' He was wincing now. Then she noticed the blood. It was turning the water red around them.

'I'm shark bait.'

'Not funny.' She spun her head in all directions. Ruben was already driving the boat to their side. Mr Ponytail and his girlfriend were hovering on the jet-ski, yelling at each other.

'You could've *killed* him, Trevor!' the girl was screaming.

For one sickening moment Trevor looked as if he was going to hit her.

'Hey, it's OK,' Sara called out, aware of Esme watching it all.

Trevor reined back his hand, as though reconsidering his violent outburst. The dolphin was nowhere to be seen.

Ruben helped Fraser onto the boat and Sara hauled herself up after him. Blood was spilling down Fraser's right thigh and calf to the floor. She hurried to grab some towels, and when she turned back she saw he was lowering himself to the floor, leaning against the side of the boat. The bulk of him was heavy as he rested on her shoulder for a moment.

Esme got to her knees, concern written all over her face. 'What's happening?'

'We have to get the coral out of me before I turn into a reef,' he told her, bringing his leg up and holding it around the calf. Esme looked stunned, but the blood didn't faze her.

'Esme, go and sit with Ruben,' Sara said, pulling the waterproof bag towards her and unscrewing a bottle of water.

Fraser winced as she dabbed at the cut. Blood was gushing from the wound, soaking the towels.

'You're cut up pretty badly—you might need stitches. Ruben, take us back to the shore as quickly as you can.'

'I'll be OK,' Fraser insisted. 'We'll just clean it and bandage it for now. You need to take your turn.'

Was he serious? 'Are you *insane*? Fraser, we need to get you back…'

'Sara, I'm fine.'

'You could have *died*!' She was pouring alcohol onto a cloth from the medical kit but the words made her choke. She paused with the cloth in her hand. 'I could swear I saw him hit you.'

He caught her wrist, right before she could apply the alcohol. 'You're shaking,' he whispered, so Esme couldn't hear them. 'Sara, the jet ski hit the rope, not me. It didn't touch me. I saw it coming and I got out of the way. I just went too deep onto the coral. I'm OK.'

She snatched her hand away. 'You almost weren't.'

She pressed the cloth to his wound, catching the blood as it continued to trickle down his calf. He sucked in a breath. He was right. She *was* shaking.

The phone rang and Fraser pounced on it. She listened as he said, 'OK, thanks…' in a way that didn't even hint at what had just happened to him. Her heart kept on thudding erratically.

'The restaurant's reported a couple of complaints this week,' he said. 'They're shutting down while they fix their air-con.'

'Oh, that's not good.'

'Well, at least no one else on the ship ate there; they've accounted for everyone and no one is showing any symptoms. The good news is that it's not the *Ocean Dream*, so we're in the clear.'

'Can we do anything?'

At the question Sara turned to see Mr Ponytail, still bobbing at the side of the boat. His girlfriend was quiet now, but she had a face like thunder. Had they been arguing before this accident had happened? Was that why this guy had been distracted?

'You can be more careful next time,' she told him, pulling hydrogen peroxide from the bag. 'Go back to the ship—we're fine here.' She mixed it with fresh water and started flushing the wound. 'And I suggest you stop these public displays of…whatever it is…on the ship. You don't know who's watching.'

'Pot, kettle, black,' Trevor replied quickly, looking between them.

Fraser scowled as Sara's cheeks flamed and the couple sped off.

There was still no sign of the dolphin.

CHAPTER TWELVE

FRASER STUDIED SARA'S suturing handiwork on his tanned leg. The stitches looked a bit like a constellation, he mused, observing the shape and doing his best not to bunch up his face in discomfort.

'Looking good, thank you,' he told her as she placed the gauze and needle beside the bed and pulled off her gloves. 'What would I have done without you?'

'You'd probably have a coral reef starting to grow in your leg. Esme believes you about that, you know.'

He swung his body from the bed, sitting on the edge of it. His limbs were achy and tired. He knew he'd be bruised tomorrow from the force of the blow.

'You'd look quite cute with a little Nemo swimming around you,' she said, packing up the medical kit. 'Still, you were lucky it wasn't worse.'

'I know.'

'I don't know what I was thinking.' Sara paused and looked at the carpet. 'I shouldn't have even been out there, Fraser. What if something worse had happened to me? What would Esme have done?'

'You can't put your entire life on hold because of what might or might not happen, Cohen. You were having a good time out there before the accident, weren't you? We all were.'

She dropped the bag on the bed beside him. 'Yes, but that doesn't mean I can run off and be irresponsible whenever I choose.'

'You weren't being irresponsible. That stuff is called living your life.'

She was quiet, contemplating the notion.

He reached for her hand, moved the bag and sat her down next to him on the bed. 'All this to see a dolphin.'

'What is up with that couple anyway?' she asked. 'Do you think there's something dark going on there? Whenever I see them they're arguing.'

'I know,' he said. 'If not loudly then really, really quietly in a corner somewhere, which is worse.'

'Much worse,' she agreed. Then she looked at him. 'We don't do that, do we?'

He grinned, and she clearly couldn't hide her smile either. 'I should probably go,' she said, a little reluctantly.

'Maybe you should.' He kept his hand over hers on the bed, then turned her head towards him. He could barely conceal what she was doing to him, being so close right now on the bed.

He shifted, turning his body towards her, ignoring the pain as it ripped through his leg. He hadn't wanted Renee to walk into the medical centre and see him like this, so they'd come straight here, and now he was finding it impossible not to touch her.

'Don't move just yet,' Sara admonished, standing up.

He saw her eyes drift over his bare torso, felt the energy course between them as she wrestled visibly with her own desires.

It had started to rain outside. He could hear it pattering on the circular windows. The ship was swaying, even though they were still in port. They weren't leaving for another day, when they'd be cruising on to Antigua, but in bad weather a lot of people tended to stay on the ship, where they knew food and shelter were guaranteed.

'I have a job to do.' She still wasn't moving.

'You're not on duty for another hour.'

'This just…isn't a good idea.'

'I happen to think it's a very, *very* good idea. See how stressed you are? We can easily fix that.'

Sara bit back another laugh as he urged her to stand between his legs. 'You're making it way too easy to be distracted,' she said.

'I was hoping you'd say that.'

He put his hands to her waist and pulled her even closer. Hang doing nothing more than kissing—they wanted each other, didn't they? He'd wanted her since the second Anton had phoned him and recommended her for the job on the dialysis team. They didn't have to sleep together just yet. But he didn't mind if they upped things from PG a little.

Sara narrowed her eyes in front of him. 'I'm supposed to be keeping away from you…this…'

'Who says so?'

She was silent, then she rolled her eyes. 'Me, I suppose. And Renee. She knows something's up between us and she doesn't need any more encouragement.'

'Something's definitely *up*,' he said, casting his eyes for the briefest of moments down to the red shorts he was still wearing.

She laughed, and groaned again, but didn't exactly object when he put both hands beneath her ass and pulled her swiftly onto his lap. In fact her legs wrapped around him instantly, as did her arms. For a second he forgot the stinging pain still shooting around his stitches.

Her palms came up against his cheeks before moving to his hair. She gripped it in bunches and let out a deep sigh as she pressed her head to his. 'What am I doing?'

'Anything you want to.'

He ran his hand through her damp hair as her knees sank into the bed either side of him. He wanted her so badly. He'd seen genuine fear in her eyes when she'd faced him in the water after his accident. She'd been trying not to show it, taking control and switching to nurse mode almost instantly, but he could read her changing moods like chapters. They'd never stop caring for each other, no matter what happened or didn't. The love they'd felt clearly hadn't gone away—it had simply been locked up for a while.

Her knees gripped his middle, straddling him on the bed, and it was she who kissed him first.

They'd used to kiss like this for hours, but they didn't have hours right now. In minutes their clothes were on the floor. They were still kissing wildly, running their hands all over each other on the bed, when a flash of pain made him wince and crumble.

Sara scrambled off him quickly. 'Oh, God, your stitches—are you OK?' She looked traumatised. 'I'm so sorry.'

'I'm good,' he managed, even as he throbbed all over... and not just from the stitches.

She was laughing now a little—embarrassed, maybe—standing on the floor in just her blue bikini bottoms. 'You need to start the antibiotics,' she told him, leaning over him again on the bed and putting a hand to his chest.

Her cheeks were red and flushed. They'd been about to make love; he'd been about to get a condom. He brought his hand to her face, urging her back down on the bed, but pain flashed through his leg again and he grimaced.

'Fraser, I'm telling you—at least take an ibuprofen.' Sara stood back, started pulling on her clothes. 'I'm going to get more bandages—I have to re-dress that.'

'No, you don't.' He breathed through the pain as it stabbed like knives.

'You're so stubborn.' She buttoned up her dress, shooting him a wary look. 'Anyway, I know we do this to each other, but it's not a good idea, Fraser—you know that.'

'No, I *don't* know that.'

'God, I don't even know what I'm *doing* after all this time. I keep making this mistake...'

'This is not a mistake, Cohen,' he told her resolutely. His leg was throbbing. If only she would stop with this nonsense.

'Don't tell yourself these things are *mistakes*. You're allowed to have some fun, aren't you?'

She froze.

'That's not what I meant,' he added quickly. 'I mean, yes, we have fun, but...'

'It doesn't matter.'

She wriggled her flip-flops onto her feet and swept her hair up onto the top of her head in a messy bun. She looked and sounded tired, more than angry.

'Call this fun, if you want, Fraser. Call it whatever you want. It doesn't matter anyway, does it? Once we leave this ship we're never going to see each other again.'

Fraser stood. He was naked now, right in front of her, and he didn't miss her eyes sweeping his entire body before she closed them and appeared to restrain herself.

'Start the antibiotics,' she ordered, turning for the door. 'Or that's going to get worse.'

He strode ahead of her quickly, through a surge of pain, and put a hand to the door, keeping it shut. 'You really think I'd be doing this with you if I never wanted to see you again?'

She looked away, gnawing on her lip now, at his shoulder height.

'Sara, please talk to me.'

'I don't see how we even *could*, Fraser. Our lives are completely different now. You're going back to your surgery in Edinburgh; I'm taking Esme back to London...'

'Why do you always have to make excuses?'

'What do you mean, *always*?' She blinked at him. 'It's not an excuse. It's the truth. I have a sick daughter who needs me every hour of every day that I'm not working, and sometimes even when I am. I can't just gallivant around the world when I get home, doing what I like, where I like, with *you*. I need a plan.'

Guilt raged through him as she moved his hand from the door. He opened his mouth to tell her about the plan—the plan he'd set in motion. The plan that might not make it to fruition, which would then make her feel even worse. He shut his mouth again.

'I'll see you later,' she said, kissing his cheek, then flinging open the door and leaving him standing there, naked.

He hopped back behind it, wary of unsuspecting eyes. She was driving him crazy.

He crossed to the coffee table, where his laptop was open, pulling on his shirt and boxers as he went, being careful not to aggravate his stitches. Dropping to the couch, he dialled into the ship's private Internet connection. Only a few people had access and he was one of them. Maybe it would be here now—the good news he'd been praying for.

He pressed 'inbox', and when the messages had downloaded—surely slower than when the Internet had first been invented—there it was, finally.

It was not good news.

The transfer centre needed something else from him. Luckily he could sort it out once they reached Antigua, but it meant he couldn't take antibiotics. He couldn't have them in his system if he had to do more tests.

Frowning to himself, he pulled on clean shorts, wincing at the pain. This was the toughest job he'd ever had to do.

CHAPTER THIRTEEN

'So, I'm going to tell you about my robo-kidney,' Esme explained.

Marcus was enthralled. He'd been waiting patiently for the chance to see what made Esme so special since the start of the cruise. It had been tough finding the time and space to entertain him in the dialysis unit, but Sara had promised Esme.

'First I weigh myself. Today's weight is sixteen point five. Then I take my temperature. Ninety-eight point four, which is good.'

Sara smiled to herself. Esme was enlightening Marcus as best as she could about all the wires and tubes and beeps. Her daughter knew the procedure by heart, of course—something that impressed Sara and pained her all at once. Would there ever be a day when they wouldn't have to go through this?

'Then they take my blood pressure, and a little bit of blood from my lines. They hook me up to the dialysis machine.' Esme patted it with one little hand. 'Which is what they call my robo-kidney. See these two tubes?' She pointed at them, one by one. 'The red one takes the blood and the machine cleans it, and the blue tube puts the blood back in.'

'So why can't you eat ice-cream?' Marcus asked. His brow was furrowed as he stood there studying the dialysis machine with interest, looking at all its buttons and tubes.

Sara masked a small laugh, putting a hand to his soft brown hair. After all this technology and machinery; and after seeing Esme's catheter and lines every day, still all the kid really cared about was why she couldn't eat ice-cream.

'No one should eat ice-cream in the middle of the night—especially when they're supposed to be in their beds.'

'Dr Fraser!' Esme trilled in delight as he appeared in the doorway.

Sara had her back to him, but at the sound of his voice, all the hairs stood up on the back of her neck.

'Hey,' she said, turning around. He stepped into the dialysis room, holding up a hand. The sight of his tall, broad frame made her heart start to beat a little faster under the harsh lights.

'What's going on in here, Spielberg? Where's your camera?'

'Mummy says I can't bring it into the dialysis room any more.'

Fraser's blue eyes fell on Sara as he stepped towards them. 'Mummy is probably right—a lot of private things occur in rooms like these.'

Sara swallowed involuntarily. She couldn't help remembering what was underneath his clothes...the way she'd left him standing naked as she'd flung open the door.

She hadn't really seen him much since she'd left his cabin the other day. The medical centre had been ridiculously busy and she'd been roped into attending a parent/child picnic and sleepover in her time off. But of course Fraser had been on her mind constantly.

She'd been ready to make love to him. She'd been caught in the moment, relieved that Trevor's damn jet-ski hadn't sliced off his beautiful head. But him being in pain had made it *not* the right time and she was glad now, because she was already getting too close to him. So was Esme.

'What's happening?' she asked him, busying herself with tidying away some equipment.

'How is your leg?' Esme asked him before *she* could.

'I had to pull three fish out of it this morning,' Fraser told her, pulling a face.

Both she and Marcus giggled. The sound made Sara smile.

Esme motioned for Fraser to move to a chair and made a thing of examining his chest with a broken stethoscope Sara had given her earlier.

Fraser looked as handsome as ever in his white coat—a look completed by his trademark sneakers, ideal, like her own, for gripping a swaying deck. His hair was less dishevelled than she'd seen it last, when she'd rammed her hands through it while kissing him passionately. There was no other word for it than passion. They'd always had that in spades.

The thought made her hot again. Damn him.

'Your heartbeat is strong,' Esme was telling him now.

'Good to hear it.' Fraser put his hand to his heart. 'Can you hear any more fish swimming around in there?'

Esme pressed the stethoscope to his belly button. 'I can hear a jellyfish!'

Fraser pretended to look horrified. 'Oh, no! What about sharks?'

Marcus clapped his hands. 'He's full of sharks!'

Sara leaned on an empty bed, watching them. 'How are the stitches really?' she asked now, stepping towards him on the chair.

'Totally fine,' Fraser said, too quickly. 'Healing nicely already. I was actually wondering if we could just...'

'Let's have a look?' Sara noted how Esme shuffled up closer to get a better look.

'I've looked plenty of times myself, Nurse,' Fraser said, clearing his throat somewhat anxiously. 'How about we check for more sharks inside me, huh?'

He went to take the stethoscope from Esme, but Sara took it herself and put it behind him on the counter. He sounded as if he really didn't want her looking at his leg. His tone had put her on guard immediately.

'Esme, go and play with Marcus—his mum is waiting outside.'

'Do I have to?'

Sara raised her eyebrows. She was surprised that Esme even wanted to see anything like this without her camera to record it. She'd told her not to film so much. She was only going to go home and make her watch all this footage of her and Fraser over and over, torturing both of them.

'Show me,' she commanded him now, getting down on her haunches in front of Fraser as the kids ran from the room.

'If you insist.'

He started rolling up his jeans. Her fingers brushed lightly through the hair on his lower calf, his warmth making her heart increase its pounding. She looked into his eyes, but he wouldn't look at her now.

Something was definitely up. She knew him too well. But she knew not to push him, too. She re-dressed the wound in silence, before the Tannoy summoned them both back to work.

'How long have you been having these headaches?'

Sara fixed the bed around the young Irishman. His fiancée had sent him in a panic after he'd blacked out on a sun lounger, and she was more than concerned for his well-being already.

'On and off for about a year. I thought they were just stress headaches, because of my wedding.'

The guy was in his late twenties. His name was Conor, and he looked guilty the second he said it.

Sara put a hand to his forehead. 'What do these headaches usually feel like?'

'Like someone's stabbing me in the frickin' eyeballs.' Conor grimaced in pain. His voice was breathy, faint. 'I haven't had one in a while, so I thought the cruise would be OK. But the casino just now…all the lights and the noise. I had to lie down. Can you give me some painkillers? I'm sure it's nothing worth wasting your time over.'

'The lights and noise made it worse?' Fraser was listening to their conversation in obvious concern and Sara met his eyes. They both knew this wasn't good.

'Sometimes I see flashes behind my eyes too.' Conor was still holding his head.

'How long have you had these flashes?' Sara asked him.

'They started a few months after the headaches did, I think.'

'Have you been to your doctor at home about this?'

'No. Like I said, with the wedding plans, and then this cruise to celebrate my mam's sixtieth, there's been a lot going on.'

'Your health should come first,' Sara told him. 'Do you drink?'

'No. I used to.'

'Why did you stop?' Fraser asked, stopping his notes. 'Did it make your headaches worse? And the flashes?'

Conor looked at him in surprise. 'How did you know?'

'Lucky guess.'

Sara watched as Fraser reached for the ophthalmoscope, stood beside the bed and shone the light into Conor's eyes one by one. When he examined his left eye, Conor cried out in pain.

'Oh, Jeez, that's worse. Can you please just give me something.'

'Worse when you look to the left?'

'Yes. Much worse.'

Fraser put the ophthalmoscope down while Sara attached the blood pressure cuff around Conor's arm. 'Have you had any other problems lately? Any pains? Any blood in your urine? Anything like that?'

The colour had drained from Conor's face now. 'Yes, a little… I thought it was because I ate too much steak.'

'Blood pressure is normal. Is it just your head that hurts right now?'

'Yes.'

'How long ago did you last see blood in your urine?' Fraser asked.

Sara instructed Conor to turn and applied pressure slowly down his left side. When she pressed lightly on his kidneys, Conor winced.

'Yeeow, that hurts! The last time I saw blood? I don't know—a couple of days ago, I think. I forgot about it.'

'I don't want to panic you,' Fraser said, keeping his voice low. He glanced at Sara again. 'But we need to run some tests. You're showing signs of polycystic kidney disease, and with your headaches combined you'll need to be checked for brain aneurysms.'

'What?' Conor looked distraught.

Sara felt her mouth turn dry. A cruise ship was no place for this poor man. Over fifty per cent of people with aneurysms died when they ruptured, and even without the test Conor, with his wedding on the cards, was showing all the signs of having one.

'What's an aneurysm?' he was asking Fraser now. 'I mean, you can treat that, can't you?'

Fraser shook his head. 'I'm not going to lie to you, pal, we can't. It's deadly serious.'

'Deadly?'

'It's a weakness in the wall of one of your brain's blood vessels,' Sara explained, putting a steady hand on his arm. 'When the blood runs through your brain, the weak spot pushes that thin wall outwards, which forms a bulge—a bit like a balloon with too much air inside it.'

Conor's eyes were round as she continued.

'If it ruptures, the blood can leak out into your brain tissue—which is not good at all. We need to get you to the hospital as soon as possible; we can't help you here.'

'Oh, Jeez, my mam will have a fit,' he moaned, seeming to forget his own pain for a moment.

It never failed to upset Sara that so many people experienced disturbing symptoms like blood in their urine and blinding headaches and still couldn't find the time to seek medical advice.

They were almost at Antigua now, and thankfully another storm had passed them by with nothing but a bit of heavy rain, enabling smooth sailing. Still, there was the rest of the day to go, and the open water wasn't an ideal location to be dealing with a suspected advanced aneurysm.

'We'll need to monitor you here until we get to Antigua,' Fraser explained as Sara went for an IV. 'You'll need to see a neurologist there for an MRI scan. You have insurance?'

'Of course.'

Sara breathed a sigh of relief. That was one good thing, at least. They'd managed to save poor Enid and her husband a health insurance nightmare by not calling for medevac, but if a situation was a matter of life or death, as this one was, they'd have no choice.

'We'll give you something for the pain, for now, but you should probably think about cancelling any flights you have booked for the meantime...'

'I can't do that. I've so much to do back home. Are you saying I might get stuck on the next island? Ouch.' Conor clutched at his skull again.

'That depends on what the neurologist there has to say,' Fraser told him, moving the IV closer for Sara. 'But you can't fly like this. You're lucky nothing happened on your flight out to the US—it might have exacerbated the situation.'

'This is a nightmare.' Conor gripped both sides of the bed as Sara hooked him up to the IV.

'We'll need to check his neurological function every few hours, and we'll arrange for an ambulance at Mount St John's,' he told her moments later, when he'd taken her aside. 'The Medical Centre on Antigua is one of the best in the Caribbean—he chose a good time to come to us…if you know what I mean.'

Sara nodded, trying not to notice again how sexy he looked, trying not to recall the way her body had almost glued itself to him.

'I'll call St John's,' Fraser said, but as he went to the telephone he stumbled slightly.

'Fraser? You OK?'

'I'm fine.'

She frowned. It looked as if it was taking every ounce of his strength not to make a sound in front of their new patient, and she could see he was in a lot of pain. 'Is it your leg?'

He straightened, held his hands up as if to stop her coming any closer. 'It's fine,' he said.

She stepped towards him anyway. 'Why are you still in pain?'

He lowered his voice. 'I told you. I'm all right, Cohen, I'm handling this.'

His guarded tone took her aback. She glanced at Conor, but he had his eyes closed, oblivious, thankfully. 'You did start the antibiotics, didn't you?' she asked. She'd held her tongue before, but this was something that could affect his work, and she couldn't let that happen here.

Fraser busied himself getting Conor's meds together. She could tell he was avoiding her. Come to think of it, he had been avoiding her ever since it had happened.

'Fraser, you know as well as I do that that was a deep wound. Just because you didn't get wiped out by that jet ski, you're not invincible, you know. What's going on?'

'Nothing.'

'That's not true. I know you, don't forget.'

He stood in front of her, closer, blocking her from Conor's eyes—not that the lad could hear from where he was. 'The meds make me feel queasy,' he explained. 'I don't need that on a ship that could be caught in another storm any second.'

She frowned, putting her hands on her hips, then quickly folded them when she realised she sounded and probably looked like his mother. This man was driving her crazy.

CHAPTER FOURTEEN

FRASER LOCKED HIMSELF into his cabin and sat at the laptop. He had to be quick. Sara was monitoring Conor, who was worrying both of them—not that they were telling the guy's fiancée that.

Jude was such a sweet girl, with her wild red curls and freckled nose. They were very young to be getting married, he thought to himself, grimacing again with the pain he'd been trying and failing to hide all day. Then again, if you loved someone, why waste precious time? He'd wasted enough of that himself, living without Sara.

She could call their encounters 'mistakes' all she wanted, but he was damned if he was letting her go again at the end of this cruise without a fight.

The glare of the computer's light filled the cabin. He found himself holding his breath as the emails downloaded, as slowly as ever. He hated hiding this from her, lying to her. He'd never been seasick, ever. He just had to wait a little bit longer.

Boyd had explained in a previous email how his intern had somehow misplaced his original urine test. Fraser had been too agitated to read or remember the finer details, but thankfully this email confirmed that he now had an appointment scheduled in Antigua for another one.

He let out a sigh of relief as he closed the email. 'How can you lose a urine sample?' he muttered to himself for the thousandth time. But he remained grateful that, wherever he was in the world, people could help him.

Another email drew his attention. This one too was from Boyd, fresh in his inbox.

Fraser, I wanted to send you a personal note about this.

I have a couple of things to attend to at the hospital in Antigua this week. I'd like to meet you there and talk to you about something else while you're there. There have been some interesting results concerning your blood tests that I feel we should discuss before going any further.

No need to panic, but I think we need to sit down in person.

See you soon,
Boyd

Fraser read the email again, anxiety making him restless. What did he mean 'interesting results' concerning his blood test? Fraser had performed his own blood tests; he knew he was clean. Whether or not he'd be a match for Esme was a different story. What if this delayed things even more?

He tried not to feel disappointed. Of course these things took time—that much had been explained to him numerous times. He sat back on the couch, running his hands through his thick hair.

He wanted to tell Sara everything about his plan, right now, but if he did her mind would be elsewhere while she was working, and that wouldn't be fair on her, or Conor, or on any of their other patients. He didn't doubt her ability to focus in an emergency, of course—he'd seen that side of her countless times—but he didn't want to rock the boat, so to speak.

What if he wasn't eligible at all?

What if all this was for nothing?

It was all making him feel far more queasy than the ocean did.

'Fraser, are you there? We need you back here, ASAP.'

Sara's voice on the airwaves sounded worried. Standing

up, and ignoring the shooting pain in his leg, he grabbed the radio.

'Conor's getting worse,' she told him, the second he stepped back into the medical centre. 'He kept saying it was the worst headache yet, then he described the sensation of having a flush of water over his head. Eyelids drooping. Double vision.'

Conor's fiancée Jude stepped aside to let Fraser through. She was panicked to say the least. Her cheeks were as red as her head of flaming red curls. 'What's going on? Why is this happening?'

'Wait outside, please,' Fraser told her quickly, taking her elbow and ushering her to the door.

'Please, let me stay,' she begged. Her big green eyes were pooling with tears.

'It'll help us do our jobs better if you wait outside.'

'We'll let you know what's happening when we have some news,' Sara told her.

Jude left reluctantly. He could see her shadow outside as he went back in and picked up the phone.

He watched Sara work as he started to co-ordinate with the Coast Guard's flight surgeon. If Conor had experienced any bleeding into the space between his brain and surrounding tissue it was bad news. There was nothing they could do on the ship about a subarachnoid haemorrhage, if that was what he was experiencing. It was likely he'd need a lumbar puncture.

'This is serious, and we're still fourteen miles from land,' he said into the phone. 'Yes. There *is* a risk to life, limb and eyesight. He's breathing, but his blood pressure is rising.'

He caught Sara's questioning glance. His words must be worrying her and he knew it.

'It's OK,' Sara whispered to Conor at his bedside, though Fraser was pretty sure that at this point Conor couldn't hear her. 'Help is coming.'

He was put on hold. He caught Jude peeking through the

glass of the door and his heart went out to her as Sara applied the pressure cuff again. Ruptured brain aneurysms were fatal in roughly forty per cent of cases like Conor's, and even if a patient survived, over sixty per cent experienced some sort of permanent neurological deficit.

No one could deny that waiting till the ship reached land would at this point be putting Conor's life even further in danger, but Fraser knew full well that there was a certain hierarchy involved when it came to a Coast Guard deciding to perform a medevac.

He glanced to the window. The sky was getting darker as the world outside inched into twilight, and the wind was picking up again.

'They won't send help?' Sara asked him as he stood there, still on hold. She walked over to him. Concern was written all over her face. 'We really need them here *now*.'

'I know.' He held a hand over the receiver. 'But sending a helicopter medevac is viewed as being a last resort,' he whispered. Her perfume smelled like lilies. 'The Coast Guard knows we're pulling the ship into port soon; also that we have competent medical staff on board.'

'But there's only so much we can do in this case.' She was clearly trying to keep the horror she was experiencing from her voice.

He held a finger up to his mouth. Someone was back on the line.

'Yes, yes…' He paused, looking to Sara. 'Yes, we can provide a professional.' He paused again as Sara's eyebrows shot to her hairline.

She motioned to herself with a pointed finger. 'Me?'

Fraser nodded his affirmation and watched her let out a deep breath, obviously trying to compose herself as he carried on making the arrangements.

'They're on their way,' he said when he hung up. This time he placed a hand at the small of her back and led her to the side of the room. 'Are you OK to go with him? They need a nurse from the ship.'

'Yes, of course,' she told him, flustered.

Conor was out cold.

'Are you sure? The helicopter medevac team are only equipped with the basics. If he needs more, which he likely will, we have to sacrifice a member of the ship's staff.'

'Of course—of course I'll go. But what about…?'

'Esme will be fine. Don't you worry. Jess is here, and Marcus, and me.' Fraser put a firm hand to her shoulder, forcing her eyes to meet his. 'I'll prepare Conor for evacuation. He'll need extra blankets—it could be a cold and bumpy ride. Go and get your things together—warm clothes for you too. I'll get a message to Jess and tell her to meet us on deck.'

'Do you think he'll make it?' Her fear was evident.

'I don't know,' he said honestly.

Sara pulled on jeans and a red cardigan, the warmest things she had with her for a Caribbean cruise. She packed an *Ocean Dream* backpack with clothing for the night and made her way to the deck. The beating of her heart was the loudest thing in her head, but she heard Fraser before she saw him.

'Out of the way please!'

He was making his way over to her quickly. His broad shoulders were highlighted by the ship's lights, which were also shining on Conor, lighting the scene of the emergency for the helicopter. It was controlled chaos.

The bright yellow bulk of the medevac was a whizzing beacon in the sky. It couldn't have been too far away when they called, thank goodness. Sara felt angsty for a million reasons. And she couldn't see Esme yet.

'You all set?' Fraser stopped in front of her, his sneakers almost touching her black flats. 'Are you OK with this?' His hair was wilder than ever in the wind. His white coat was thrashing about his frame. He leaned in closer, speaking over the noise. 'This is about as exciting as these cruises get, Cohen.'

'You're telling me.'

'You'll be fine.'

His fingers were twitching at his sides, as if he too was finding it hard to resist reaching out to her before she was hoisted into the sky.

'I'll meet you at the hospital as soon as I can.'

'I'll take care of things,' she said, pulling her cardigan round her tighter as the helicopter inched ever closer over-head. 'Where's Esme?'

Fraser was being called on the radio. From the corner of her eye she registered the arguing couple again. The black-haired girl was shoving Mr Ponytail's chest with her palms, angry at him about something as usual.

She should probably talk to that girl at some point, she decided. But she couldn't think about that now.

'Mummy!' Esme was rushing at her from Jess's side, run-ning across the deck in her pink pyjamas. 'Mummy are you really going up in the 'copter?'

Sara reached for her, scooped her up into her arms, breathed in the scent of her warm hair. 'Someone is very sick,' she said. 'I have to go with him to the hospital. I need you to be brave and do what Jess tells you, OK?'

'Can I come?' Esme asked in a small voice as she put her down.

Fraser crouched down to Esme as the wind whipped at their clothes. 'This is something Mummy has to do for work. She has to go and be a superhero—is that all right with you?'

Esme studied him. 'Yes…' she said cautiously, after a moment.

Renee was with Conor, talking over what was happening and what was about to happen with his family as the staff prepared a special stretcher for the airlift.

Sara would have to be raised along with him; there was no way the helicopter was landing on the deck. So surreal.

Fraser caught her bag as it threatened to blow from her shoulder. The rotor blades were drowning their voices already. Esme watched the helicopter with fascination, one hand locked in Fraser's, her camcorder focused on the scene. Sara didn't have the heart to tell her to turn it off. She'd probably never seen anything so exciting in her life.

She kept her head down the whole way over to the stretcher. They'd loaded Conor up and were making space for her beside him. Time was ticking. In reality it had only been a few minutes, maybe seven or eight, since they'd made the call to the Coast Guard, but under such pressure it felt like an eternity.

She said a silent prayer as Jess came for Esme and Fraser took control of the situation. She followed his every command as she was buckled and strapped.

'Make sure Conor's head is supported…make sure his tubes are wired and not about to blow away…make sure he's covered in yet another *Ocean Dream* blanket.'

He was already covered in at least six.

She looked up at the paramedic, readying himself to be lowered onto the deck, and tried not to think what might happen if the winch broke.

'Stand back, please!'

Security were in action around the deck, stopping those passengers who were moving about the scene with their cell phones.

Her breath caught in her throat as the paramedic started lowering himself on the line towards them. He was swaying in the wind, his bright orange jumpsuit turning him into some kind of exotic emergency bird.

'Please help him…we're getting married,' Jude sobbed. Her bright red curls were being flung in all directions by the wind and the helicopter blades.

Sara felt for a moment as though she were floating above the scene, rather than a part of it.

In seconds she was lifted into the dark sky. She caught her

breath as the wind threatened to steal it. Fraser's eyes were on her. She could still see him from above, on the deck with his hand above his eyes, shielding his face from the bright lights.

She was a professional—she could deal with this. But as the ship became a strip light in the distance, and the endless sky stretched before her, just the thought of him and Esme *both* being so far away was terrifying.

CHAPTER FIFTEEN

CONOR HAD NEEDED seven and a half hours of surgery to clip the aneurysm in his brain.

'He opened his eyes and asked if we'd started the surgery yet,' the surgeon said.

Fraser watched as Sara lowered her head beside him. She was exhausted—that much he could tell. Her eyes held shadows he hadn't seen before.

They can't let him die. Please, we're getting married,' Jude had whimpered on their way over to the hospital from the port.

He could see her now, through the glass, sitting at Conor's bedside. She looked calmer, but her desperation born of fear had snapped off another piece of Fraser's heart that was always reserved for his patients.

He couldn't help wondering what Boyd was about to tell him regarding his blood test. His concern had escalated, and all the drama combined had meant he hadn't slept a wink either.

'The fact that he came to us when he did, and that he was in your care when it ruptured, saved his life,' the surgeon said now to Sara. He was twiddling his long grey beard with two fingers. 'It didn't cause any irreversible neurological injury.'

Sara looked relieved. 'Thank goodness for that.'

She was still in her clothes from last night, which were crumpled at best. Her long cardigan looked cosy, like something he wanted to snuggle against with Sara still inside it.

'It was a blessing that the Coast Guard was so close,' Fraser said. 'Any further away and they might have written off our case. Conor certainly wouldn't have survived if they'd waited for the ship to reach Antigua.' He looked to Sara. 'Not a bad result for your first medevac.'

She threw him a weary glance. 'Thanks to *you*, Fraser.'

'Take a compliment. We make a pretty good team.'

He noticed her smile, albeit a little tightly, no doubt thanks to her tiredness.

Conor was blinking groggily. Jude was clutching at one of his hands. His mother, nearly forty years wiser, was clutching the other one even harder.

'You should go and get some sleep,' he told Sara, thinking of his own mother for a moment.

He still felt guilty every time he left her, even after two whole years without his father being around, though she insisted she was fine in that big old house all alone.

'I can keep an eye on things here for the next couple hours, sort the records.'

'Are you sure?' Sara swiped a hand over her eyes and forehead.

'Of course I'm sure. There's some other stuff I have to do here anyway,' he told her, stepping aside with her. 'I'll meet you back at the ship?'

He hoped she'd agree. His appointment with Boyd was set to commence on another level of the hospital any minute now. He would have had to come here anyway, of course. He just hadn't planned on Sara being there, too.

'I've spent enough time on that ship,' she told him, taking him by surprise. 'Esme's going on a trip on a glass-bottomed boat. Isn't there something fun *we* can do, Mr Tour Guide?'

She crossed her arms and looked up at him expectantly. Conflict took him hostage. He wanted nothing more than to spend some down-time with Sara, but this was a strange day in general.

'You don't want to sleep?'

'I'll do that later.'

In her eyes Fraser saw a glimpse of the playful girl he'd fallen for back in Edinburgh. 'Not if I can help it,' he said softly, before he could stop himself.

A laugh escaped Sara's mouth. She reined it back in behind her hair and turned it into a yawn as the surgeon turned to them questioningly.

'OK,' Fraser said. 'If you want to do something fun, meet me at the beach I told you about the other day? You remember the one?'

She raised her eyebrows. 'I remember. Two hours, OK?'

'That should be long enough. Bring Esme, if she's back from her trip.'

'What do you have to do here anyway?' she asked him. Her face held a sombre expression now. 'Did you bring someone else from the ship?'

'No, it's just admin. See you soon—I might even buy you an ice-cream.'

Fraser took the stairs two at a time, stopping to help an elderly lady into a wheelchair on his way.

'Such a handsome darling,' she said, and grinned at him through gappy teeth.

Fraser saluted her as he hurried on his way.

Passing the dialysis clinic, he recalled the brand-new idea that had sprung into his brain and refused to go away over the last few days. He'd been pondering over opening a dialysis unit at the Breckenridge Practice. Maybe Sara would help him run it. It was just the kind of business decision his father would have approved of—a way to grow the practice into something more, with far-reaching potential.

He couldn't wait to be able to talk about it all with her. Hopefully after this second test, and whatever it was concerning Boyd about his blood tests, their prospects would at least be a little clearer and he could maybe even reach the beach this afternoon with good news.

'Dr Fraser Breckenridge?'

The Caribbean woman who opened the door to him was

probably eighty-five. Her white coat came down to her feet, which were in rather scuffed trainers.

'That's me,' he said, amused. 'I'm looking for Dr Boyd Phillips.'

'He'll be back soon. He's asked me to take another urine test first.'

'Fair enough.'

She opened the door to let him inside the tiny, somewhat stuffy room. He couldn't help remembering, in the face of this elderly nurse, the time a younger Sara had called him for tests before his marathon—the playful Sara, who was slowly but surely coming back to him in spite of her reservations...

'Fraser Breckenridge?' Sara had looked up as he'd closed the door to the white and too-bright room. 'Here for your tests?'

He'd stepped inside and noticed her hair: long, blonde, but not the tacky kind of blonde, the kind that was natural and always looked good messy.

'Yes, that's me,' he'd said, shutting the door behind him. 'Thanks for doing this. I know you probably have something more interesting to do.'

'I can't think of anything more interesting than this.'

Sara Cohen had almost perfectly symmetrical eyebrows that were real, not drawn on with pencil, and her words had held no trace of sarcasm. She'd scanned some papers. Her nails were pale purple.

'So you're running a marathon, huh?'

'Indeed I am. As long as I'm innocent on the inside.'

He had smiled serenely with what he'd hoped was suspicious purity. He hadn't known why yet, but he'd wanted her to wonder about him.

Sara had raised her perfect eyebrows. 'You don't strike me as the innocent type.'

She was teasing him. His interest in this woman was mounting. Sure, he'd seen her about the hospital. She was pretty, friendly—nothing to write home about...or so he'd thought. She was great with the kids. All the kids at the hospital loved her—almost as much as they loved him.

She'd leaned against a cabinet with one hip and eyed him in a way that had made something stir in his jeans. Her tight fitted white coat ended just above her knees and her shoes were dark blue velvet flats, as if she was planning to ballet dance away from her nursing duties. She was graceful.

He had wondered what she looked like naked.

'Well, there's a lot you don't know about me,' he'd told her.

'Apparently so.'

'I know about you, though. I've seen you knitting.'

It had come out before he could think. He was usually able to play it cooler than this.

She'd lifted her eyes from his running shoes up to his face. 'What does that tell you about me?'

'It tells me you're either pregnant with triplets or you just really like knitting… OK I don't know about you. I think I want to find out, though.'

He'd rested his backside on the back of a chair. Had seen a battered copy of *Lord of the Flies* sticking out of a satchel on the floor by her chair. He'd seen her reading too, in the canteen. Big novels like this. He'd never told her, but he'd read every single one of the books he'd seen her reading long before.

He liked this little game they were playing, and he liked Sara too, with her butterfly earrings and her fondness for literature, and shoes he could picture her dancing in…naked.

But he couldn't get distracted. He really needed this drugs test.

'Listen, I need these results back pretty quickly, if that's OK?' He'd stood, looked up around him for the container. Surely she would have it ready.

Sara had opened the drawer by her hip and pulled out a container with a small white lid. 'We're all set.'

'Sperm sample?'

She'd held the container out to him carefully between two

fingers, slightly away from her body. 'You know very well we need a urine sample,' she'd said. 'For now.'

The more he'd grinned, the more her own lips had twitched at the corners. He'd seen the laughter fizzing in the colour of her irises. The way she'd said 'for now' had been unmistakably flirtatious.

'Do you need a drink of water first?'

'I'm good—thanks for caring.' He'd stepped a little closer, pressed his hands into his denim pockets so as not to touch her.

'In that case,' she'd said, lowering her voice in mock seduction, 'the bathroom's through there, Fraser Breckenridge.'

They'd been inches apart.

'Maybe when I'm done we can go get some lunch?' he'd ventured.

'That depends on how innocent you are.'

Fraser had held her gaze, more than slightly aroused ahead of his bathroom visit. So *this* was Sara Cohen. If this *had* been a sperm test, he'd probably have no problem right about now...

CHAPTER SIXTEEN

'ALL DONE?' BOYD motioned Fraser through into another room and into a chair on wheels by a desk.

'Let's hope it's second time lucky.' Fraser took his seat in the stark white room, trying not to show how the anticipation was messing with his head.

'Apologies for the mix-up with the urine sample,' Boyd said. 'I hope it wasn't too much of an inconvenience.'

'Not at all,' he replied, just because it was polite. 'So, what is it you want to discuss in person?'

Boyd sucked in a breath and let it out slowly. He took off his big round glasses and dangled them from his fingers over the desk, all of which put Fraser's nerves even more on edge.

'Boyd, what have you found?'

'It's interesting,' he replied, sitting back in his chair, studying him. 'Fraser, how long have you known Esme, exactly?'

'Since the start of the cruise we're on,' he said. 'Why?'

Boyd slid a piece of paper across the desk to him. 'Fraser, I don't want to alarm you, but did you ever think there might be something that her mother isn't telling you?'

'What do you mean?' Fraser took the paper in his hands. 'What am I looking at, Boyd?'

'The blood tests show you're a perfect biological match to Esme. Fraser, this kind of blood type is so rare you're possibly the only person who *could* be her donor.'

Boyd tapped his finger on the piece of paper. The letters

and numbers blurred before Fraser's eyes. He could hardly believe what he was hearing.

'I don't understand...' He did, but it didn't seem possible.

'Fraser, Esme appears to be your daughter.'

The world seemed to skid to a stop. All he could hear was his heart pounding in his ears. When he looked up Boyd was still studying his face in concern.

'This can't be true.'

'I'm afraid it is.' Boyd rested his arms on the desk, still holding his glasses. 'I hate to be the one to break this to you, Fraser, but either Sara doesn't know herself or she's been keeping it from you. I think you need to have a talk with her before we go any further. No matter what the new urine tests show...'

'This is crazy, Boyd.'

He stood up, strode to the window, raking his hands through his thick hair. Palm trees waved at him from under a blue sky, but all he could see was Esme's face, and Sara's too.

'It can't be.'

'I understand this completely changes things. It must be quite a shock.'

'That's an understatement.'

Fraser turned around again and paced the small room, drumming his fingers against his thighs as the world shifted around him. Anger. Denial. Shock. Some strange new hope. It was all bubbling inside him now.

He sank back into the seat heavily, took the piece of paper again. He blinked as unexpected tears pooled in his eyes, and embarrassment made him slam the paper down again hard.

'How could I not have known this, Boyd? All this time.'

'You say you've been apart for five or six years, right? With no contact? Did you ever try to make contact?'

'Only once, about two weeks after we broke up.'

He stared unseeingly at the desk, remembering Sara standing there with her one-night stand. Whatever had happened, she clearly hadn't wanted a man around to help her with a baby, and from what she'd said to him so far, the way she'd been pushing him away, she was wary of having one around now…

This was more than he'd bargained for. He was a *father*? He had a *daughter*? A sick daughter he'd missed out on knowing all this time.

He took the paper and got to his feet again.

'Fraser, take some time to think about this,' Boyd said calmly.

But Fraser was already striding for the door.

CHAPTER SEVENTEEN

'Honey, what are you doing?' Sara rushed across the sand to Esme. 'You can't do things like that. What's the problem?'

The little girl whose sandcastle had just been unceremoniously bulldozed by Esme was screaming the beach down, pulling a total tantrum in her pink two-piece swimsuit.

Sara took Esme's wrist and led her aside gently. She was always gentle, no matter what. 'Baby, tell me—why did you do that?'

'She told me I was going to die!'

White heat, all over her.

Words like this tore her to pieces. She composed herself as Jess appeared in her giant yellow hat. They'd been having such a nice time until now.

She crouched down and put her hands on Esme's little waist over her cotton sundress. 'Esme, you're not going to die.'

The kid's mother was walking over now, wearing sunglasses far too big for her face. 'What happened?'

'I'm so sorry about that,' Sara told her.

She was starting to wish she'd gone back to bed, like Fraser had suggested; she was far too tired for all this. Come to think of it, where was he? He was supposed to have been here twenty minutes ago.

The woman spoke loudly, haughtily, over her screaming daughter. 'I don't know what kind of parent lets their child—'

'Excuse me?' Sara stood rigid.

The woman shut her mouth. She was looking at Esme's

catheter. Her face had turned slightly pale, like everyone's did when they started viewing Esme less as a child and more as some precious flawed person who might keel over and expire at any moment. Her illness brought out the best and the worst in people all at once at times. Other mothers with healthy children suddenly felt guilty, or woke up to the fact that they were blessed.

This woman seemed particularly ashamed. 'I'm so sorry. I didn't see…'

'That doesn't excuse her from being naughty,' said Sara.

'She told me I was going to die!' Esme cried again.

'If you cross over the *bridge*!' the kid in pink insisted, pointing to the smashed elements of her creation. 'I told you—you only die if you cross over the bridge! You smashed my bridge!'

'It's only a game,' Sara told Esme. 'She was including you in her game. You're not going to die. She didn't mean it like that.'

'Where is Dr Fraser, Mummy?'

She looked at her helplessly. 'I don't know, sweetie. He's supposed to be here…'

'What *is* that…thing?' The screaming child had stopped her tantrum and stepped up close to Esme, inspecting the lines running up from the neck of her white dress.

Here we go again.

Esme swiped at her eyes. 'It's my catheter. I'm on dialysis. I have a robo-kidney, and you're right. I might die.'

Sara wrestled with the need to flop down onto the sand and close her eyes. She took a deep breath and let Jess lead Esme away from the drama towards the shoreline.

'You are *not* going to die,' she whispered after her anyway, and the horrible woman, now sufficiently apologetic if only with her eyes, slunk away, back to her sun chair.

Another half an hour passed. Esme was happily building sandcastles again, but still there was no sign of Fraser. She watched the waves lap the shore, seeing his eyes and the way he'd looked at her that time when she'd asked where he'd been in Florida. He wanted to tell her, he'd said, but he couldn't yet.

She'd made peace with that, and even grown to believe he was planning some kind of nice surprise for her. But he'd skipped out on her again now, when he knew she'd be with Esme. When he knew Esme would be disappointed if he didn't show up.

Annoyance bubbled into anger. She was back on that staircase, feeling what she'd felt the first time her thoughts about Fraser Breckenridge had weighed her down rather than lifted her up.

She'd flown back to Edinburgh six months after they'd started dating and three weeks after her mother's death. Just to be near him. She'd felt bad for leaving her father, but her sister had been with him and both of them had told her that she should go and do something nice for herself.

They'd eaten dinner an hour after she'd arrived—Sara, Fraser and his parents. All the way through their perfectly *al dente* pasta his father had looked between them, as if he was dying to get something out in the open. It had been after dinner, on her way back from the bathroom, that she'd heard them talking.

'She's no good for you, son. You're in danger of screwing it all up. What about your career? What about everything you've worked so hard for?'

His voice had made her shiver. And what had been worse was the fact that Fraser hadn't defended her or their relationship. That fact was the knife that kept on stabbing her in the heart, every time she thought about that night.

The rest of the evening had been awkward. She'd made her excuses, gone upstairs to his bedroom. Fraser had come in when she'd been sitting on the bed, staring at the floor, knowing her heart was about to be torn into even more pieces.

'What are you doing up here?'

'Just thinking.'

He sat down on the bed beside her. 'OK… Well, I'm glad I've got you alone. Listen, I was hoping we could talk.'

She had struggled to breathe as his hands had left dents on the bed either side of him. She'd already known what was coming. He was going to end their relationship.

'You know I need to qualify this year, Sara. You know the practice needs me. So…'

'You don't need to explain, Fraser—honestly. I've been thinking I should talk to you, too.'

She'd stood up then, paced the room while the lump in her throat had caused her physical pain. 'This is just such a bad time. My dad really needs me… I shouldn't even be here.'

'Sara…'

'We should call it a day, Fraser. It's just too crazy right now…everything is changing. Under the circumstances I think it's best. I'm so sorry. I shouldn't have come here.'

Her taxi had sounded its horn outside and Fraser had stood up in surprise, yanked the curtain aside. 'What the hell—?'

'That's my cab to the airport.' She'd reached for her bag.

Fraser had walked up to her purposefully, making her gasp as he snatched the bag back and held her by the shoulders. 'Sara, what's happened? Why are you saying this? Talk to me.'

But she'd pulled away, reached for the bag she had already packed. 'Fraser, we've just been delaying what you know needs to happen. I don't belong here. I need to be with my dad and my sister in London. And you need to be here.'

His mouth had been a thin line. His fists had curled to his sides. She'd been convincing enough.

'It's what I need right now,' she'd continued, though her tears had been coming thick and fast. 'I should go.'

She hadn't been able to keep on talking. Her heart had been hurting too much. But she hadn't been able to stick around for him to break up with her either.

Whether he did it now, or next week, or next month, he was going to do it eventually. His family and career meant too much to him for her even to try to keep a place in it right now. She'd leave quickly, like ripping a sticking plaster off, before the real pain of a deeper wound could kill her.

She had cried the entire way home...

Sara blinked at the beach scene in front of her. They were building more drama around themselves now; she could feel the weight of it, making her sink again. And when it came to Esme she couldn't allow herself to sink, or even to float passively along. She couldn't wait around for anyone to prove themselves to her—not him, not anyone.

Gathering up her stuff, she called to her daughter and headed to a small boat bobbing on the waves. A skinny guy with dreadlocks was arranging water skis on the back of it, checking the fuel tank. As she bartered for a deal she forced herself to feel excited, to focus on Esme and to give her a memory she'd remember for ever—however long that was.

'Where's Dr Fraser?' Esme asked again as they zoomed out onto the ocean, just the two of them.

'He's busy.'

'Doing what?'

'It doesn't matter.'

'Is Dr Fraser a daddy?'

Sara's heart lurched beneath her lifejacket. 'Why do you ask that?'

Esme just shrugged, staring out at the waves.

'If you want to come back, remember to pat your head. If you want me to cut the motor, act like you're slashing your neck with your hand.'

They were bobbing now and adrenaline was making her knees knock as the driver got everything into place.

She glanced around for jet-skis. There weren't any in the immediate vicinity. Her mind flashed to Trevor and his girlfriend. She would find them and talk to them as soon as they got back to the ship. Again she'd let Fraser distract her from what she needed to be doing; something wasn't right with them.

The driver started up the boat. Esme started her camera rolling. And Sara had no choice but to do what she'd been adamant she would do...with or without Fraser.

She moved slowly at first, till she caught her balance... then faster, till she felt as if she was flying.

It was a rush, a total thrill when she managed to stand, and when the boat and the driver and Esme were so far ahead that she couldn't make out their expressions any more.

Her knees were bent, her arms were straight and her head was up, facing forward, with her hair flying out behind her.

'Whoo-hoo!' Esme hollered from the boat.

Sara could see her now. 'Whoo-hoo!' she hollered back. 'I'm doing it!'

For the next half-hour or so Sara fell, got up and went again, over and over and over again, until she was buzzing from head to toe. She was a strong, capable woman, able to do things by herself. Fun things.

How many more experiences like this could she squeeze into this trip before she'd have to go back home...? Home to where Esme would be stuck again, waiting...waiting for what?

Was she really going to die?

Her thoughts began to whirl with the wind, like tsunamis rushing past her ears. Fear, loss, guilt. Annoyance that she still couldn't get Fraser and his deeply upsetting absence out of her head.

She fell—hard.

She crashed into the water like a bomb, face-first, in a move so undignified that she was quite shocked. Her life jacket kept her afloat as soon as she slowed, and she was on her back, blinking her salty lashes at the sky.

It was only then that she realised her face felt as if someone had punched her.

CHAPTER EIGHTEEN

SARA WAS STANDING by a bed when Fraser arrived, tending to a woman called Jasmine who appeared to have broken her foot or her ankle. The young girl with black bobbed hair, in too-short denim shorts, was sucking in breaths as if it really, really hurt. She had a very large bruise surrounding her right eye, but he recognised her instantly.

She was the girlfriend of Mr Ponytail—one half of the couple who seemed to be permanently at each other's throats. Trevor...that was his name. Did he even remember the way he'd almost killed Fraser with a jet-ski?

'She told me she slipped on the bathroom floor,' Sara said, but the look in her eyes told him something else was going on—just as they'd suspected from the start.

His jaw pulsed as she stepped up close to him and pulled him aside. Speaking of bruises, at least Sara's face was looking better than before.

He'd been pleased she'd gone water skiing on her own, but he'd told her right there and then, after she'd tracked him down to ask why he hadn't come to the beach, that something had happened. He'd told her that they needed to talk—but not till they'd left the ship for good.

Then he'd shut the door in her face and reminded himself that they didn't have long till they left the ship, so he'd do as she had first requested and stay professional, while he processed this life-changing news and while Sara went back to ensuring his daughter was having the time of her life.

'She's not saying much,' Sara whispered. 'I went to talk

to her last night. I told her she had to get away from any situation that was causing her distress. Trevor came back to the lounge and heard me.'

'This isn't your fault.'

'He probably got angry at her...'

'This is *not* your fault.'

He turned away from her before he touched her, or pulled her out of the room and asked her how the hell he had a daughter after all this time. Those big eyes could always make him crumble. So could Esme's. And now he knew why.

He had a daughter. It was killing him, keeping it inside. But it was for Esme's sake that he had to for now.

Sara was talking quietly to Jasmine. Trevor was staring at him from the plastic seat in the corner, nervously wringing his hands on his lap. His trademark ponytail was dangling limply down his back like the tail of a dead cat.

Fraser held out his hand to him. 'Dr Fraser Breckenridge—I believe we've met already.'

'Yes, hi...' He sounded awkward. 'I'm...'

'Trevor. I know. What happened? You say she slipped?'

Jasmine was doing her best to straighten herself on the bed without adding any pressure to her leg or ankle. Sara hurried to stop her.

'Yes, I slipped.' Jasmine said it with a clenched jaw and a quick glance at Trevor which told Fraser pretty much all he needed to know. She was covering for him.

'Any more pain?' In his peripheral vision, he saw Sara going for the X-ray machine.

'No, not really. Just the entire leg now.'

'We're going to help you—don't worry,' Sara said, wheeling it over.

He helped her prep it and adjust Jasmine, and as they took the X-rays he wished to hell that he could see inside Sara's head, too.

Of course he wanted to talk now, but waiting for the right place and time was vital. It was better than raising their voices in an emotional confrontation, if it came to that, or having to spend the rest of their time here working together when…when she might have been lying to him for years.

He literally couldn't stand the thought.

'Nothing else hurts,' Jasmine said now as he continued checking her over.

'What about that mark on your face?'

She looked away. 'It's…it's nothing. That's an old bruise.'

'It doesn't look old,' Sara said.

'Well, it is.'

'Well…as far as your foot goes it looks like a sprained ankle, but we have to be sure it's not a fracture.'

Jasmine's ankle was swollen to about three times its regular size, and was already turning a nasty shade of grey, ringed by an angry purple.

Fraser took over while Sara helped her to get more comfortable, stabilising the suspected fracture site with a pillow splint. Trevor still looked anxious. He kept standing up and then sitting down again on the hard plastic chair in the corner, twiddling his ponytail and his fingers.

'Do you want to wait outside?' Fraser asked him.

'No. I want to be here with Jasmine.'

'Just go, Trevor,' Jasmine's voice was weary as Sara adjusted a pillow under her head.

'Wait outside, please,' Fraser said sharply.

'Why?'

'Just go. I'll be out in a second.'

They all flinched when Trevor slammed the door behind him.

'What were you doing when you slipped?' Fraser asked Jasmine quietly.

'I told Nurse Cohen here—there was water on the bathroom floor. The pain shot up my leg…sharp, it was, like someone with a chainsaw was inside it… Then it all went numb. He had to carry me here.'

'We'll give you something for the pain,' Sara said, 'but,

Jasmine, you have to tell us the truth about what happened. Covering for him won't solve anything.'

Jasmine bit her lip, but refused to say anything more.

'You have a lateral malleolus fracture—that's a fracture at the end of the fibula, right here,' Fraser informed her minutes later, once he'd looked at the X-rays. 'Luckily your tibia is OK. Nurse Cohen, would you prepare a cast?'

'Of course.'

'We'll have to get you crutches, I'm afraid, Jasmine, and put you on some painkillers. They'll make you more comfortable. I'll be right back.'

Outside, he folded his arms in front of Trevor. 'I've heard you and Jasmine arguing before now. And I have to ask: does this injury have anything to do with an argument?'

Trevor stiffened and mirrored his stance with his own arms. His biceps were covered in black and white tattoos.

'What are you implying? She slipped in the bathroom—she already said that.'

'What happened to her face? It's not an old bruise. I know what a fresh bruise looks like.'

Trevor looked directly into Fraser's eyes with his small beady blue ones, then appeared to bloat with pure, unadulterated anger. 'Why are you asking me all this anyway?' he yelled, waving his arms in the air. 'Your job is to fix her foot and nothing else. What gives you the right to ask about my personal life?'

Fraser didn't budge an inch. 'Please don't raise your voice to me. With all due respect, this is part of my job.'

The door opened and Sara stepped outside. 'Dr Breckenridge?'

'Everything's OK,' he told her.

'Jasmine seems pretty shaken up over something,' she said, looking at Trevor now. 'More than just her ankle, maybe.'

'You're *still* going on about this? Seriously?'

Trevor seemed outraged at her presence, and made to step

towards her. Instinctively Fraser put an arm between him and Sara, and held his hand up to stop him.

'Is this because of the jet ski thing?' Trevor seethed. 'It was Jazz's fault anyway—she was telling me to go towards the dolphin!'

'Would you please lower your voice?' Sara said.

Fraser stepped slightly in front of Sara. 'Trevor, tell me, is there anything else you want to tell us about what happened to Jasmine today?'

Trevor made an obnoxious snarling noise and then stormed off away from them.

'He shouldn't be left alone,' Sara told him.

'I'll keep an eye on him.'

Fraser headed for the elevator, frowning. He knew Jasmine hadn't simply fallen in a wet bathroom, so why on earth was she defending Trevor? He couldn't get his head around it. But he was no psychologist, and who knew how hard the heart fought the head in those situations? How many couples put up with months, even years of arguing and abuse out of fear or out of love?

He couldn't even imagine getting so sick of someone that it got to the point of physical abuse; he'd never been in a relationship like that in his life. He would only ever love Sara Cohen—and, more than that, their daughter.

CHAPTER NINETEEN

'SO, WHAT'S HAPPENING with you and that sexy Dr Brecken-ridge?' Jasmine asked as Sara prepared her cast. Her voice was the kind of faux chirpy that spoke volumes about her pain.

Sara pulled on latex gloves, resting a bowl of cold water on the table by the bed. 'We just work together,' she said. She steadied Jasmine's raised ankle and separated a pile of fibreglass strips. 'I'm more interested in what's happening with you and Trevor.'

'Nothing's happening. Like I told you before, Trevor is just a bit crazy sometimes. You've seen it yourself—he almost killed your boyfriend. He blames me for everything.'

'With his voice, or with something else?'

Jasmine looked away.

'It's OK to tell me. It will go no further than you want it to,' Sara said.

She picked up one of the strips and dipped it in water. The water started to swish a little.

'He *is* your boyfriend, isn't he? Dr Breckenridge? We had a bet, me and Trevor.'

'How long have you two been together?' Sara kept her voice low and calm, applying the strip over the padding. Jasmine was not going to quit.

'Me and Trevor met at college—it's been five years too long now. You didn't answer my question.' She was drumming her nails on the bed now, doing everything she could

to distract Sara from the issue at hand. She seemed to har-
bour some deep-rooted fear of getting Trevor into trouble.

'Nothing is happening with me and Dr Breckenridge.'

'Nothing?'

Sara sighed as she worked. She wished she *could* talk
about it to someone. There had been something serious and
unrecognisable in Fraser's tone, and in his eyes too, when
she'd found him that night…when he'd told her they had to
talk but only once they'd left the ship for good.

It had chilled her to the bone. But she respected that whatever he had going on, if it was that serious, it made sense
for them to talk later. They were working together, after all.

She considered that maybe someone on the ship had spoken to him about them and he didn't want to embarrass her.
Or maybe he'd finally woken up and realised that Esme was
getting too close to him, that she herself was carrying too
much baggage. She was afraid now even to approach him
about that. She knew she wouldn't actually be able to stand
to hear him say that and then have to work beside him without being able to get away. He was right—maybe they did
need some space.

Jasmine had been watching her laying the strips. But now
she said, 'I don't believe there's nothing. I can practically feel
the flames coming off the both of you. I've seen him playing with your daughter, too. I thought she was his for a bit.'

'No, she's not his,' she replied, laying another strip across
Jasmine's calf.

Jasmine lay back down again. 'We saw you all together
on that boat. Is that stuff allowed when you're working on
these cruises? Don't they get all funny about staff hooking
up unless they're married?'

'I don't know.'

Sara's brow was perspiring slightly under the fan. The
gentle pattering sound at the windows had turned to heavier
rain. The ship was moving with what felt like a lot more pur-

pose too—up and down, up and down. She could feel it in her stomach again, like the night they'd lost Esme.

Jasmine was looking at her expectantly.

'It's...complicated,' she told her. 'Keep still, please.' She moved the swishing bowl of water closer, worried that it might tip over.

Jasmine groaned. '*All* relationships are complicated.'

Sara considered her words. 'Is yours? Tell me how you really got that bruise.'

'I told you.'

'Tell me the truth.'

'There's nothing to say.'

Sara's reply was cut short by a huge crash of thunder. It ripped through the room, through the walls, and made Jasmine almost jump off the bed. She yelped as her ankle slipped from its support and the bowl of water went flying.

Sara hurried to reposition her. 'Sorry—try to stay as still as you can. Can you believe this weather?'

'They said it would rain, but this is actually a bit scary. I *knew* we should have paid for the good season cruise.'

Jasmine clutched at the sides of the bed as Sara retrieved the bowl and ran fresh water. She carried on with the cast as quickly as she could, while the rain lashed even harder at the circular windows. She caught sight of the sky through the glass for the first time in hours. It was a deep, dark grey, verging on black.

'You'll have to stay here for now,' she told Jasmine when she was done. She snapped off her gloves, moved the bowl of pasty white water to the sink. 'Dr Forster will be in soon to monitor you. If you touch it, please just use the palms of your hands—we don't want you denting it, OK? That could irritate the skin under the dressing and you don't want to be left with sores and scars.'

She crossed to the cupboard and took out some crutches. 'Usually we'd wait forty-eight hours or so to move you, but with weather like this we'll leave these here just in case.'

Another strike of lightning lit the sky outside.

'Will I be able to fly home when we get to Florida?'

Sara paused with the crutches. 'With Trevor?'

Jasmine shrugged.

'Jasmine, I would advise against going anywhere with him after this.' She gestured to her cast. 'You're not fooling anyone—or yourself, I'd imagine. Do you really want to spend your life with someone who treats you like this? What if you say nothing and he does it to someone else?'

Jasmine closed her eyes, balled her fists.

'You should be able to fly just fine if you can get an upgrade that allows for more leg room,' Sara said, her tone softer this time. 'But we're stopping in Puerto Rico first— how would you like to say goodbye to him there?'

'That wouldn't be a good idea.'

'Why?'

Jasmine was still clenching her fists. 'He hits me.'

She said it through gritted teeth, as if even getting the words out finally was painful.

Sara laid her hand on her arm. Thank God she'd admitted it. Tears were glistening in Jasmine's eyes now; she was clearly terrified.

'He won't hit you any more,' she said resolutely, 'whether he stays on the ship or not. We can help you out of this.'

'Don't tell him I told you anything. Please, don't tell anyone—not on the cruise.'

Sara's heart was breaking for her. 'Why? What do you think he would do?'

The thunder crashed outside again. Jasmine clammed up and refused to say anything else.

It worried her, and so did this storm.

CHAPTER TWENTY

On the top deck, Sara found a few merry passengers vacating the outer decks, carrying plates of food inside. She assumed the others were already far too seasick. There was no escaping the rain either—not even under the deck's huge umbrellas. Through the windows in the corridor she saw a giant potted plant slide right across the deck in the lingering twilight.

Where was Fraser? She had to tell him what Jasmine had said so they could figure out what to do together. She'd said nothing to Renee when she'd arrived, reading the pleading look in Jasmine's eyes, but she couldn't risk another act of violence on Trevor's part.

Renee had slipped Sara an all-access key card before she left. Everyone knew anyway.

They had to alert someone. Fraser had gone to find Trevor, so maybe they were in Trevor and Jasmine's cabin. What was it Jasmine had told her for the charts? Cabin 202.

Knocking on the door, she had trouble standing up. 'Fraser, are you in there?'

She clutched at the doorframe, hoping Esme was still OK downstairs, watching cartoons with Marcus and his mum.

'Fraser? Trevor?'

There was no answer. She swiped the key card, but the room was empty. Curiosity got the better of her and she stepped into the bathroom. It was clean, with no sign of blood. But that didn't mean anything.

She headed for Fraser's suite. Security had ordered everyone to stay in their cabins, so she couldn't imagine where else he would have gone. Besides, Fraser's cabin was big, and he likely had Security in there with him, figuring out what to do with Trevor in private. With Jasmine's confession they could get the law involved more easily.

She let herself in, feeling strange as she did so. 'Are you in here?'

His cologne lingered in the air. A pang of longing struck her core as she saw the bed. There was no one here.

She stumbled to the bathroom just as another lightning bolt struck the ocean outside the circular windows. 'Fraser?'

Maybe he'd come back alone.

No, he definitely hadn't.

On the way out she saw it—something she hadn't noticed before on the table by his laptop. She crossed to the couch and picked up the pile of photos.

The sight of Fraser's mother in one picture took her by surprise. She looked older than Sara remembered, by more than six years. Grief would do that to you, she thought sadly. Dropping to the couch at another lurch of the ship, she flicked quickly through the rest.

She knew what she was looking for even before she found it.

Holding up the photo of her and Fraser, she couldn't help smiling at the memory. They'd been at a gala ball, a month after they'd started dating. She was wearing the butterfly necklace he'd given her. He'd always said this was his favourite photo of her. It was slightly ruffled round the edges now.

He probably missed that old Sara, who'd had nothing to worry about but books and stupid butterflies.

Something else caught her eye. An official-looking document, sticking out from beneath the laptop. The heading was in big black and red type: *Florida Transplant Institute*.

Her pulse quickened as she gripped the table-top. What the hell was she doing? This was Fraser's private stuff and she had no business going through it—and besides she had to find him.

On second thoughts…a transplant institute?

Pulling the paper from beneath the laptop, she realised she was shaking. Something deep in her bones was telling her this concerned her and Esme, so much so that she could barely read beyond the address of the institute…

Beep-beep.

The door to the room sprang open. Sara's heart almost crashed through her ribcage. She leapt up from the couch, holding the piece of paper behind her back quickly, feeling it flapping against her under the ceiling fan.

'What are you doing in here?' Fraser stood stock still in surprise in the doorway. His broad frame almost filled the corridor.

'Looking for you.' Her voice was strangled as he moved towards her, his eyes narrowed now. He'd seen the photos, no doubt laid in a different place than he'd left them.

Sara moved away from the coffee table. 'Jasmine told me,' she managed. 'She just told me. Trevor hits her.'

Fraser was still looking at the photos. 'I thought as much. Trevor needs to get off this ship ASAP. He's downstairs with Security. Jasmine's safe with Renee now, right?'

'Yes.'

'Good…good job.' He crossed to the fridge, grabbing a can of Coke.

Her fingers trembled around the document. She knew beyond all shadow of a doubt that whatever she was holding behind her back was what Fraser had been hiding, and what he had shut her out from. She gripped the arm of the couch with her other hand and sat down again. It was hard to stand upright.

'They're probably going to be ready for him in Puerto Rico, as soon as this storm's over.'

She swallowed. 'To do what?'

He held out the Coke. 'To arrest him, Sara—what do you think? What's wrong?'

He stepped closer to her, suspicion written all over his face now. She was acting weird, and she knew it. She stood and made to step away, around the table, but a jolt from the ship made her stumble against him.

The piece of paper drifted to the patterned carpet and Fraser's eyes followed it.

'I didn't mean to see it,' she said quickly as he slammed down the can and picked it up. 'I didn't read it—just the header. But, Fraser, why do you have a letter from the Florida Transplant Institute?'

The rain was pounding at the window. He held the paper in his hands and seemed to look straight through it to the floor. His voice was strained when he spoke.

'I wanted to wait till we were off the job to talk about this,' he said, dropping it to his side. 'I told you that. I wasn't planning to hide anything from you.'

'Wait for what? Fraser, is this about Esme? Did you find a donor?' She couldn't disguise the hope from her voice. Her heart was thrumming.

Outside, the wind was howling.

'Maybe.'

'Maybe?'

'I just thought that there might be few things you need to tell me first.'

His voice was different now—not angry, just loaded, filling her with fear at the fact that she couldn't quite read him.

He put the paper back down on the table. She racked her brains. 'I don't know what you mean, honestly. What do I need to tell you?'

'You honestly can't think of anything?'

'No, Fraser—stop being so cryptic and just tell me!'

Pain flashed in his eyes as he looked at her, and it made her feel ill.

'I went to the Florida Transplant Institute to see about donating a kidney myself,' he said.

Her hand flew over her mouth.

'I didn't want to tell you unless I knew I could do it, Cohen. I know you said Esme has a rare blood type, for a start, and that the chances are slim. I wanted to be sure I was eligible before giving you anything else to worry about.'

She was silent as his words sank in. The swaying of the ship and his news were both making her queasy now.

'Esme is my daughter, Fraser—did you not think I had a right to know?'

'Of course I think you have a right to know. I just didn't want to put any more pressure on you while you were working. I wanted Esme to have a good time while you were here…'

'Esme? Fraser, I asked you where you were that morning.' She felt light-headed. 'You should have just told me then.'

'I know, and I'm sorry.' He sat down next to her. 'This hasn't been easy. I was trying to do the right thing, believe me. But, like I said, if there's anything you need to tell me, please just do it now.'

She shook her head at him. The Coke can slid across the table. There was only one thing she could possibly need to tell him, and she couldn't think how he'd found out. Why did it even matter now, anyway?

He was looking at her imploringly.

'OK,' she said. 'OK, Fraser—yes, I broke up with you because I overheard what your dad said to you, and I *had* to do it first. You didn't even defend me, or us, and I didn't want you to hurt me any more than I was already hurting over Mum.'

'What are you talking about?' He got down on his haunches in front of her, put a hand to her knee. His hair was falling into his eyes.

'I broke up with you because I *knew* you were about to do the same thing to me. Fraser, you have to admit you would have done it eventually. Is that why you didn't try and talk to me when you saw me with someone else in London? You knew I was better off without you while you worked to get your career on track?'

Fraser dragged his hands through his hair, shaking his head. He looked genuinely perplexed.

'I heard your dad say I was no good for you,' she continued, more warily now. 'He said you were in danger of screwing everything up, everything you'd worked so hard for before I came along.'

'You overheard my father talking to me?' Fraser's eyes were incredulous spheres.

'Yes, after that dinner. And I heard you say absolutely nothing in my defence.'

'Sara, you only heard half of it!' He stood up and the ship swayed, making him crouch back down and grip the table. 'They wanted me to finish my studies with no distractions, so I could release the money my grandfather left for me in the family trust fund as quickly as possible and pump it all into the surgery. They were going broke!'

'Broke?' She didn't understand. The Breckenridge family had always seemed extraordinarily wealthy.

'I was completely backed into a corner. I had to do what they asked. I was too ashamed to tell you what the situation was really like… I was young and too proud maybe. I don't know.'

'Too proud? To tell me your family were in financial trouble?'

'Yes, and to tell you *I* was in trouble with my studies. I was juggling it all fine for a while. Until I wasn't. I would have told you—maybe even that night. I tried to talk to you, remember?'

'I only remember being confused…'

'We should have talked to each other. I wanted to work something out, so I could be there for you, *and* get back on track, *and* fix the family mess too. But you broke things off before I had the chance. And then you slept with *him*, Sara.'

Sara just stared at him, speechless. All this time and she'd never known. She could feel a headache coming on. It was both their faults, then, their break-up: the doomed result of a series of grief-related bad decisions and general miscommunication. They'd been so young, and so much had been going on all at once.

'Cohen,' he said now. 'Whatever you heard, whatever was said, none of it meant you had to hide Esme from me.'

She blinked at him, her mind a carousel. What on earth did Esme have to do with anything that had happened back then?

'You had no reason to get involved with Esme,' she managed. 'Fraser, I appreciate what you've done, trying to help me, but you don't need to be getting involved with Esme's battles—at least not without talking to me first. Esme is my number one priority—you know that. She's *my* daughter, after all.'

She saw his jaw twitching, as if he wanted to say so much more than he was saying. Then the thunder cracked again and he got to his feet.

'Listen,' he said. 'Go to your cabin, please, where it's safe. When the storm passes I'll come and get you.'

She panicked, sensing a gap wider than ever opening up between them. If it wasn't this that he thought she needed to tell him, what was it?

'You need to talk to me *now*.'

'We'll talk later. I need to go downstairs and tell them what Jasmine has said.'

'I'll come with you.'

'No, I don't want you around Trevor.'

'I can handle myself.'

'Please,' he said, softer now. 'Sara, I'm saying this because, despite everything, I still love you.'

He was already reaching for his jacket.

His words had stunned her. *Despite everything?*

'Go and find Esme,' he said. 'Stay with her.'

'She's with Marcus and his mum...she's safe,' she heard herself say. Her ears were roaring at his words—all of them. 'Wait, Fraser, I don't want you to think I'm not grateful for what you're trying to do.'

'We don't know for sure yet if I'm eligible. I'm just waiting on one more test result that's got delayed.'

'I can't believe you're doing this. *Why?*'

'If you don't already know,' he said, pulling on his jacket, 'now is really not the time for me to tell you—trust me.'

The Coke can rolled completely off the table.

Fraser paused in his exit, seeming to compose himself. He strode back over, leaned down with his arms either side of her on the couch's back, and kissed her.

'You're scaring me now,' she said, bringing her palms to his cheeks.

'I love you,' he said again. 'You know I do.'

He pulled away, then headed for the door.

'We'll talk later, I promise. Just stay where it's safe.'

CHAPTER TWENTY-ONE

'WHAT'S HAPPENING?' FRASER walked into the medical room to find several items on the floor. Renee looked flustered and Jasmine was in tears.

His head was reeling the more he ran over everything, and he didn't have it in him to think straight, let alone get into the issue of Esme being his biological child with Sara.

Another fact was slowly sinking in: the fact that she had broken up with him in Edinburgh as a result of overhearing half of a stupid conversation. If she hadn't… If she'd only spoken to him, and he to her… They'd both messed things up.

But he couldn't think about it now. The ship was bucking wildly.

'Grab that!'

Renee called to him to catch the X-ray machine as it slid quickly in his direction. He stepped over a rolling pill bottle and fixed the machine back in place behind a steel counter.

Renee walked to him unsteadily even on flat shoes. 'Fraser, there's a situation on deck.'

'What kind of situation?'

She lowered her voice as he stood on a rolling plastic cup. It crunched under his foot before he picked it up.

'Someone's up on deck in the storm and they're refusing to come inside. Security are on to it.' She flicked her eyes to Jasmine and back. 'I'm not sure, but I think…'

'Trevor.' He cursed under his breath. He'd left him with Security, while he'd rushed to attend to a kid who'd been struck by his overzealous brother wielding a tennis racket.

The boy had needed nothing more than an ice-pack, but everyone was going nuts, cooped up inside.

'When was the last time you saw Trevor?' Renee asked.

'Ten minutes ago. He was with Security. They're meant to be watching him till we get to port, but he kept on saying he needed to do something, and we don't technically have any right to keep him in one room.'

'What did you say to him?'

'I told him Jasmine had confirmed he'd been hitting her.'

Fraser's jaw was clenched. He'd also told the staff not to let him out of their sight, so Trevor must have used some grand excuse. Or demanded to use the bathroom and slipped off somehow.

There was a loud crash, just outside the room. Jasmine shrieked. Fraser yanked the door open to find a painting from the wall face-down on the floor. An ashen-looking woman in a purple robe was staggering down the hallway towards him.

'Come in here,' he said, hurrying towards her, gripping the railing as he went.

The woman was moaning and tripping over her robe, clearly in agony. Sara appeared just as he was helping her.

'I told you to stay in your cabin,' he said. 'I said I would come and get you later.'

'Don't tell me what to do—I want to help,' Sara said, bristling.

'Get her a bedpan,' he told her, too busy to argue.

He swiped the rolling pill bottle from the floor and Sara took the woman from him and led her to a bed—just as she threw up on the floor.

'Stay in here,' he said now, to everyone in the room. 'Don't come out until you hear it's safe. I'm serious, all of you.'

'Where are you going?' Sara looked up, her eyes narrowed as she held the woman's hair back.

Their new patient's purple robe was trailing in vomit. Jasmine was still crying.

'To the deck,' he said. He didn't wait for any protests. He didn't have time, and he wouldn't have listened anyway.

'Dr Breckenridge—you can't go out there!'

A security guy tried to stop him on the top deck. He recognised him from before.

'I'm medical staff and this is an emergency—I need to go out there. You weren't supposed to let him go.'

A crowd of people were gathered around the windows with cameras, ignoring the command to stay in their cabins. Did *anyone* follow orders on this ship?

'The ship was tipping. I only took my eye off him for a moment and he made a run for it,' the security guard explained.

'Let me go out there.'

'It's not safe...'

Fraser thrust open the door. He was faced with the swirling ocean, a blackened sky. A blast of wind shot inside the ship and tugged at his jeans and white coat. He shut the door behind him, leaving the security guy struggling to stop a man following him out with a camera.

The sea spray lashed at his face, but across the deck he could see shadows in the rain. They were bulky, broad-shouldered. Some of the security team had followed Trevor at least.

He made to move towards them, but each motion was like wading through a swamp. Every time he tried to move the wind would blow him backwards and pain shot through his leg. He pushed it away as best he could; he still hadn't taken the damn antibiotics.

Then he saw what the security men were looking it.

Trevor's long wet ponytail was swaying like a rope in the wind. His tattoos were disappearing along with his neck, head and shoulders as he took small steps backwards into the darkness.

'Don't do this!'

A member of Security was holding his hands up. Another shone a flashlight into Trevor's face. His T-shirt was a flapping flag as Fraser forced his legs to move forward.

'Trevor, let's go back inside.'

The howling wind took his breath. Trevor didn't move. He clearly had something terrible planned.

'I have to do something.' Trevor was as white as the moon.

'Not this. Listen to me. You don't need to do anything drastic.'

'Yes, I do.'

Fraser saw his eyes flit to the edge of the deck and the heavy lounge chair standing strong against the gales. The perfect ladder.

'I promise you, you don't,' he called.

'My dad used to hit me, you know.' The flashlight on his face showed his beady eyes filled with despair. The fury was gone.

A call for help.

Fraser had seen it before from people like this with secrets to hide. Secrets that were hurting them and others.

'Let's go back in and talk about things.' He inched closer to Trevor in the seconds when the wind died down. At the same time Trevor leapt onto the lounge chair and stepped up to the edge.

Security men rushed forward, but Trevor lunged for a rope and pulled himself up high, away from their arms' reach. He was teetering on the edge now, holding on tight to the swaying rope over the pounding ocean.

'Fraser!'

Fraser spun round. Sara's white coat was a billowing sail. She had one arm around Jasmine, who was staggering towards him on crutches.

He caught her before she toppled. 'Her plaster isn't even set properly!' he yelled.

Jasmine held a hand up at him. 'Don't blame Sara—I

begged her to bring me!' She clocked Trevor, who was still clutching the rope. 'Trevor, please, get down from there!'

The wind and rain was whipping round them now.

'There's something bad inside me, Jazz…it's in my blood.'

Trevor was clearly distraught. Fraser forced himself to say nothing that might push the guy literally over the edge, but he reached for his radio—slowly.

'No!' Trevor saw him. 'Don't you dare!'

'Fraser, stop!' Sara looked appalled. 'He's going to jump.'

Jasmine was whimpering between them.

'OK… OK…' Fraser shoved the radio back. 'Trevor, why don't you just let me help you get down from there?'

He forced himself one step forward.

Trevor stepped over the side.

'No!'

Fraser got to the edge first. In a heartbeat he'd caught Trevor's arm, snatching his wrist, slippery with rain. Salt water stung his eyes, and he could barely see, but he clamped down with an iron grip and somehow Trevor swayed like a pendulum but didn't fall.

Sara was next to him now. He tried to pull Trevor higher, so she could reach him too, but Trevor's hand slipped and he had to use every ounce of his might to stay holding on.

'Please, don't drop me!'

So now he wanted to live.

Without hesitation Sara reached down over the edge, while a security man reached for her. She clamped a hand over Trevor's arm. Then she grabbed him by his shirt.

'Now!' she yelled.

The wind whipped her hair into Fraser's face as together they dragged him inch by inch, writhing and groaning, back from the edge. They all toppled backwards as he tumbled onto the deck, and Fraser crawled to Sara while Security took over. They were wrestling to hold Trevor down; he was panicked now—not wanting to die, but not wanting to be there in their control, at their mercy.

Jasmine seemed to fall to the deck and they hurried to help her up, one on each side, acting as the crutches that had rolled away. They were all soaked through.

A crowd of stubborn passengers surrounded them as they finally stepped inside.

Jasmine was concerned for Trevor as they dripped their way back to the med room. 'What will happen to him?'

'Security will take care of things,' said Fraser. 'Does your leg hurt even more now?'

'No, it's fine—I told you.' She was limping, but luckily it didn't look as if she was in any more pain than before. 'Will they have him arrested now?'

'They won't let him go this time.'

He avoided Sara's eyes the whole way to the med room. He wouldn't say it. He wouldn't say that he'd warned her not to go up there. Sara knew she should have listened.

Pain shot through Fraser's own leg. It almost made him stagger on the threshold of the medical room.

Sara spotted it instantly. 'Fraser?'

'I'm OK. Are you?'

'Yes. But your leg…'

'I said I'm fine.'

Renee hurried over to help. She'd clearly been tending to more seasick patients: the evidence was on the bed sheets. She'd told them she could handle things, but Fraser knew she couldn't—not on her own.

'What happened? she asked them, taking in their wet clothes and hair.

'What happened was that Trevor *did* try to take the easy route out, but changed his mind.' He winced as he moved.

'Let me check your leg,' Sara said, swiping her wet hair back. 'And don't say you're OK—I can see you're not.' She sat him in a plastic chair and crouched in front of him while he rolled up his jeans. 'You didn't take those antibiotics, did you?'

She frowned as her fingers traced the skin at the edge of

his coral reef wound. It was still purple, and part of the cut was bleeding again.

'You told me it was because they made you queasy,' she whispered, 'but it was because of the tests for Esme, wasn't it? You didn't want them in your system.'

He leaned towards her in the chair. 'Yes—the other test I told you about...the one I'm still waiting for...'

'You should be putting yourself first—'

'Esme comes first,' he said, watching as she dabbed antiseptic on his wound—not that he hadn't done that already, earlier in his room.

'Go and lie down. I'll take care of things here,' she said when she was done.

'You both need to go—to change your clothes at least,' Renee instructed.

Fraser looked to Sara. They needed to talk.

'Stay with me,' Jasmine said to Sara suddenly, reaching for her hand. 'Please don't leave me, Nurse Cohen.'

Jasmine's eyes were red and swollen. She clutched Sara's hand and Fraser could see in Sara's face that she was torn. Jasmine was really scared of Trevor now—scared to be around him and scared not to be.

'There are some spare clothes in the cupboard. I'll be fine,' Sara said, just as Fraser had known she would. 'I'll stay here. Go rest your leg.'

He lingered a moment longer, but other people were listening. He knew there would be no talking tonight—not while so much else was going on.

CHAPTER TWENTY-TWO

THE POLICE OFFICERS were carrying guns, as was the way in Puerto Rico—and probably most of the rest of the world now, Sara mused. She was standing in line for snacks and drinks, with her mind still running over all that had happened.

Trevor hadn't taken too kindly to being arrested and dragged off the ship by two burly police offers in black, but thankfully the situation had been handled properly and poor Jasmine was out of danger now.

She and Renee had tended to ashen patients most of the night, and she had barely slept as the ship had continued to rock back and forth. She still didn't know how she'd summoned such supernatural strength when it had come to heaving Trevor back onto the deck. But the way Fraser had looked at her…it made her smile a little.

They hadn't found time alone to talk properly yet. She knew that whatever it was he had to tell her was serious, but the knowledge that he might be close to being able to help Esme filled her with fresh hope that overrode any fears, somehow. It was the first time she'd allowed herself to feel this much hope. She had to keep it alive.

She looked at him now. He was seating Esme in the front row for the sea lion show. Jess and some of the other kids from the ship weren't far away.

'Don't forget the apple juice!' he called to her across the rows of happy people.

He was dressed in a green shirt and the same khaki shorts he'd danced in with her on deck. The aquarium was packed.

She was really too tired for the mayhem of it all, but she'd been planning to show this place to Esme ever since she'd agreed to work on the *Ocean Dream*.

Fraser's hand brushed hers as he took his apple juice and she sat with Esme between them.

'Chilled—just the way I like it.'

He shot her a smile that sent the feel of his kisses straight back to her. A cheer from the crowd made Esme shriek in excitement and her cup of apple slices almost went flying.

'Be careful, Esme,' she told her.

Esme rolled her eyes.

Her catheter was a reminder of what her future would still entail if Fraser *couldn't* help. Sara scolded herself. No, she had to keep that hope alive.

'Have you heard anything yet?' she whispered to Fraser. 'About the other test?'

He lifted his sunglasses to look at her. 'Not yet,' he told her. 'Please don't worry. I know it's hard not to think about it, but this is why—'

'Why you didn't tell me. I understand.'

'We'll see each other later—alone. I've made a reservation.'

'A surprise?' she asked, raising her eyebrows.

He dropped his eyes from hers. 'You could say that.'

'Mummy, look!'

Esme was jabbing the air emphatically in the direction of the sea lions now plodding onto the wet deck. Their huge brown bodies reminded Sara of heavy sacks of potatoes.

'I see them—wait till you see what they can do.'

The swimming pool was gleaming—like Esme. She noticed how Fraser's eyes lingered on her daughter adoringly as she focused in on the action with her camera.

'How much footage have you racked up now, Spielberg?' he asked Esme. 'You must have enough to make three movies?'

'A lot,' she replied, turning to him with the lens pointed at his face. 'Say something about the sea lions!'

Sara hid a smile behind her hair as he made something up about sea lions. The two of them had been chattering happily the whole way here, picking each other's brains, making each other laugh… All they did was laugh.

'Will I still see you when we go home?' Esme asked Fraser suddenly, putting her camera down. 'The cruise is nearly over.' She pulled a sad face at him.

'I hope so,' Fraser said, casting a quick glance at Sara that made adrenaline spike in her veins.

They could tell her now, if they wanted. They could tell Esme that Fraser's spare kidney might potentially be hers, that her years of dialysis, of running back and forth to hospitals and avoiding delicious things like ice-cream might soon be over.

But the words wouldn't even form properly in her mind. As much as she wanted to, she almost couldn't fathom saying them out loud to Esme after all this time. Especially as a result of Fraser's sacrifice. A flush of love for him took her by surprise and she squeezed his hand. His tanned fingers were laced through hers on her lap.

'You can come and visit me and Mummy,' Esme continued cheerily. 'I'll take you to the dialysis centre!'

'I'm sure you'd make the second-best tour guide in the world after me,' Fraser said jokingly. But he didn't make any promises.

Sara bit her lip. They'd tell her together, if the results of this final test meant he could go ahead with the transplant. Maybe he *would* come and visit them from time to time— when he wasn't stuck in Edinburgh, working flat out at the surgery.

She studied his hand in hers. She didn't want to get her hopes up regarding a new relationship, even though his declaration of love had struck her deep to her core, unleashing butterflies every time she thought of it. They both knew

Esme came first. Everything depended on her getting better. Sara would have nothing to give Fraser if Esme didn't get better. She would only be half of herself.

A pair of volunteers had found their way to the pool deck. Two giant sea lions were now performing tricks, batting a beach ball between their snouts, each perched on a wooden podium. A tall, lean man and a young girl—father and daughter, perhaps?—were being zipped into wetsuits and handed some fish.

'Why can't *we* do that?' Esme asked Fraser.

'I'd be too scared,' Fraser told her, pulling a face.

'*I'd* look after you.'

'I know you would.'

It was a strange bond that he and Esme had formed so quickly. And she couldn't deny she felt bonded to Fraser too—even more so, knowing what he was trying to do for her daughter. Not for the first time she wondered whether *they* would have had a daughter together some day, if things hadn't got so messed up.

A shriek from the poolside made Esme swing her camera round. Both Sara and Fraser stood up in their seats at the same time.

'Mummy, what's happened?'

'I don't know, baby, don't panic.'

She strained her eyes to see what was wrong. She couldn't see the man any more—just the little girl he'd gone up there with. There was motion in the water. And only one of the two sea lions was still on a podium.

'Oh, God—you don't think that he was attacked?' she said apprehensively.

Fraser grabbed the medical bag he'd brought from under the bench. The crowd was going wild now, panicking, rushing to the front to see better.

'Is anyone here a doctor?' a voice on a megaphone was booming.

'They're supposed to be friendly, aren't they?' said Fraser. 'Maybe he fell in or something.'

They looked at each other in horror. In seconds Fraser was squeezing out of their row with the medical bag, hurrying to the front.

'Where is he going?'

'To see what's wrong.'

Sara clung to Esme as she watched the green of his shirt find its way to the scene. Then she came to her senses. She motioned to Jess, who took Esme under her wing, and then followed in Fraser's path as fast as she could.

There was still movement in the swimming pool when she got to the front. Flashing her ship ID, she tore up the steps beyond the security barrier, just in time to see Fraser drop his shirt on the poolside and dive straight into the swimming pool.

The sight made her freeze in her tracks.

The lifebuoy he'd taken with him appeared suddenly in the deep blue water, which was swishing so hard all she could see was a blur beneath the surface. Her heart stood still as she forced her feet to move towards the little girl. She was no older than Esme.

'You're OK.' Sara dropped to her knees next to her, feeling water soak through the fabric of her dress instantly.

'My daddy got pulled in by...by Sammy the sea lion!'

The little girl was sobbing in heaving bursts, trying to make her way to the edge of the pool. Sara held her back. The staff were a blur now too, fetching nets and poles. The other sea lion was honking. It almost sounded like laughter, she thought with a chill.

'He'll be OK,' she said, hoping to God it was true. 'What's your daddy's name?'

'Simon.'

A woman in the blue and yellow aquarium uniform was trying her best to keep some other sea lions happy further up the deck, throwing them fish from a bucket to distract them.

'They *never* do this,' someone was saying behind her, aghast. 'What did he think was wrong with that guy?'

A hand broke the surface of the pool. Fraser emerged, clutching the kid's dad. A male staff member was at his other side and together they swam with him back to the deck. Simon was aged around thirty-five. The sea lion was still circling as they swam. It looked playful to Sara, under the blazing Puerto Rican sun, not at all threatening—but who knew what these things were capable of?

'Daddy!'

The kid was distraught now. Sara kept on holding her back. Two other staff members were running towards him with a stretcher now. Simon was motionless, pale and limp. He had a nasty gash on his inner thigh, where the sea lion had clearly made a grab for him and dragged him off the deck by its teeth.

'Help me get him up—he's not breathing.'

Fraser's commands were intended for the aquarium staff so Sara did the best thing in that moment—she stayed with the little girl. All around them people were staring, recording on their phones, just like always. She tried to block it out. A woman was calling from beyond the security barrier now, waving through.

'Hey! Baby—come here! Excuse me!'

'Mummy!'

Sara released the girl and she ran towards her mother.

'They won't let me up!' the woman said, reaching for the child. 'He's my husband. Is he OK?'

'It's safer there,' Sara told her, turning to Fraser.

His shorts and hair were dripping—not that he seemed to notice. She got on her knees. Simon was laid down flat on the stretcher. She checked his unblinking eyes, his breathing and pulse. Someone was radioing the hospital.

'I didn't think sea lions could do this,' she breathed, reaching for the Ambu bag beside him.

'They're wild animals—they can do what the hell they

like,' said Fraser, unzipping the front of the wetsuit to Simon's waist. He placed one hand over the other and started rapid compressions on his hairy chest.

Sara placed the Ambu bag over his face. Her heart was skidding. The sea lion was still swimming circles in the water, and the crowd were snapping photos so fast the flashes were almost blinding her.

Fraser's chest was rising and falling next to hers as he breathed heavily in blatant exhaustion. She could hardly believe what was happening—they weren't even on duty. But they were never off duty, she realised. It was one thing after another, twenty-four-seven.

So much for this being a working holiday... She'd had her work cut out for her right from the start.

She held Simon's head, still gently squeezing and releasing the bag. Simon wasn't responding.

'More compressions,' she said, but Fraser was already on it.

She could see in his face how focused he was, how he too was trying his best to ignore the crowds and their camera flashes. Sara resumed her prayers as she counted the compressions. Simon's wife and daughter were watching and the kid's face was streaked with tears.

'We'll need to shock him,' Fraser said now.

One of the aquarium's assistants had already called for the defibrillator to be readied in the emergency room.

Sara noticed that Fraser was limping slightly, trying to ignore his obvious discomfort as they hurried to get Simon inside on the stretcher, away from public attention. They rushed down the steps, pushing through the crowds until they reached the aquarium's ER. It was even more basic than the one on the ship.

'The ambulance is on its way,' someone said.

Sara inspected Simon's wounds. The wetsuit was totally torn around his thigh and groin. She didn't like to think what being bitten by a sea lion must feel like. She could tell it was a pretty bad wound, but it was the water that had harmed him more than anything.

'The sea lion held him down like he was some kind of toy,' Fraser told her incredulously as they moved him from the stretcher to a clean white bed. 'No one knows why. Was he carrying tuna snacks in his pockets or something?'

Sara readied the machine. Simon's wet hair and wetsuit were soaking the bed now, and Fraser was leaving puddles on the floor as he worked. He dashed his hand through his wet hair. His muscled torso was on full display and she didn't miss a female staff member eyeing him up and down as he worked.

'Charging...*clear*!' he said, putting the paddles on his chest.

Simon's muscles contracted and his limp body gave a jerk at the current charging through it.

The clock seemed to stop.

Again and again they tried.

'We have a sinus rhythm—he's back,' she announced moments later, as the machine showed a blip she'd honestly thought she'd never see.

Simon started coughing wildly. Behind her the ER room door was flung open and two paramedics rushed in with a blast of warm Puerto Rican air. Someone had also let Simon's wife and daughter into the room.

'Is he going to be OK?' the little girl asked. Her face was flushed—like her mother's.

'I think he is now,' Fraser said.

Relief was written all over his face. He seemed to remember he was shirtless suddenly, and looked around for his clothes.

The female aquarium staff member was still looking at him appreciatively. She stepped forward quickly and handed him his green shirt, gushing her praise and thanks in quick Spanish.

Sara was frazzled, hot, grateful and still slightly shocked

as she filled the paramedics in on the situation en route to
the ambulance, where the pair of them were thanked over
and over for being so quick off the mark.

'This has never happened before,' the goatee-bearded
aquarium manager reiterated outside the ambulance. 'We
think Sammy was just playing.'

'It's no one's fault,' Sara said, though some people were
leaving the park, clearly afraid of the animals. This would
not be good for business. She spotted Esme and Jess close
by, waiting for them.

'Lucky we were here,' Fraser told the manager, and she
registered a small flutter of disappointment as Fraser put
his shirt back on.

The manager turned to them as the ambulance drove
away. She was about to leave, to get Esme and go and do
something slightly less exciting, but the manager reached
for her arm.

'Can we do something for you?' he said. 'To say thank
you before you go?'

CHAPTER TWENTY-THREE

FRASER COULDN'T BELIEVE that Sara had almost refused the aquarium manager's kind offer. Looking at Esme now, reaching her tiny hands towards the dolphin's smooth face in the water, he swore he'd never seen a kid look so happy.

'Thank you for this, Fraser—this means the world to her.'

Sara was sitting on the edge of the pool next to him. The sun was twinkling in her hair and in her eyes and he couldn't help thinking she was the most beautiful woman he'd ever seen, even after all this time. Beautiful inside and out.

He swished his feet next to hers in the blue water, touching her toes with his for a second. Being in an almost empty aquarium had its benefits—though he did feel bad for the guy who'd just borne the brunt of a curious sea lion's teeth.

'I didn't think she'd ever get to swim with dolphins,' Sara told him.

'I didn't think *I* would ever get to swim with dolphins,' he said, and grinned.

He had managed to score free dolphin encounters for them, and for all the kids in Jess's care. It was going to be the talk of the cruise ship. Esme was being buoyed up by her life-jacket, as well as being held by one of the female aquarium employees. Marcus was floating nearby, waiting for his turn.

'You definitely know how to turn on the charm—you've got fans for life here.'

Sara cast her eyes to the woman who hadn't stopped eyeing him up and down since she'd handed him his shirt and Fraser nudged her.

'I prefer British nurses,' he told her, smiling as her cheeks flushed a little more.

'You think the wetsuit's doing its job OK?' Sara looked concerned again. This was the reason she'd refused the offer for Esme to swim with the dolphins at first.

'It's fine. The catheter's protected—don't worry. Look at her...she's loving it.' He picked up Esme's camera as Esme was instructed to place a hand on the dolphin's dorsal fin. 'Give us a wave, Esme!'

She did so, beaming at him with so much happiness that he couldn't help melting just a little.

'She's going to want to do this every week now,' Sara said.

'Who wouldn't?' He zoomed in close as the creature started gliding slowly around the pool, smooth and con-trolled as it had been trained to be, pulling Esme along.

In his bag, his phone started to buzz. He reached for it and moved away, leaving Sara on the poolside.

'Boyd?'

'Hey, Fraser, how's it going?'

'I'm just at an aquarium with Sara and Esme.' Sara was looking at him. His heart had started to hammer. 'Do you have news?'

'I do,' Boyd said. 'Thought I should tell you myself: your tests are all clear. You can proceed with the final tests along-side Esme when you get back to Florida—just let me know and I can arrange it. I assume you'll want the surgery at home, in London or in Edinburgh? It's up to you.'

Fraser took a deep breath, composing himself. Behind him, Esme was squealing in delight at the dolphin swim and Sara was clapping her hands. Their excitement only enhanced his own.

'This is great, Boyd, thank you.'

'Congratulations,' Boyd said. 'Did you talk to Sara?' There was concern in his voice now. 'About Esme being yours?'

'I haven't had time yet, Boyd. I didn't want to discuss it on the ship at first, but… Long story. I'll tell her everything tonight. This is great news, though. I can't thank you enough.'

Back at the pool, Sara turned to him expectantly. She was biting her nails. He looked at her face and took her hand. 'That was the transplant institute. I got the all-clear,' he said.

Sara's eyes flooded instantly with tears. 'You mean…?'

'I can help her.'

She stared at him, blinking back tears, till he put his arms around her and pulled her in close. 'We'll talk about it later—all of it, everything—just you and me,' he said, kissing the top of her head, hot with sunshine.

'Fraser, I can't believe this. Her whole life will change.' She pulled away and met his eyes. 'Because of *you*.'

He felt a rush of pride and joy and pure, pure love for both of them, but he knew he had a big conversation ahead.

He couldn't help studying Esme's features through the viewfinder when he picked the camera up again. He'd been finding himself doing this ever since he'd found out—studying her nose, her lips, comparing them to his. She was *his* daughter.

The knowledge was still baffling. She looked like Sara—that much was certain—but the more he looked at her, and the more he spoke to her, the more he saw pieces of himself in her and he loved it. He loved everything about this situation—except the fact that he'd been without her so long. Maybe now he could make up for lost time, if that was what Sara wanted after the surgery.

He was still finding it tough to imagine telling Sara that *he* was Esme's father. He was almost certain, judging by their last conversation, that she didn't know. They'd always been so careful with contraception, after all. It made sense that she'd have thought Esme was the result of her one-night stand, and never considered anything else.

He had no idea how she would react tonight. Would she be upset, or angry, or in denial once she knew? And how would Esme take it?

'It's your turn!'

Esme called him into the water as both she and Marcus and the other kids had taken their turns. The dolphin was almost smiling, as if it was waiting for this swim specifically.

He and Sara both zipped into their wetsuits. Fraser slid into the water and held out his hand. Sara's blue bikini straps were visible at the back of her neck and he tucked them into her wetsuit as she placed her hands on his shoulders. They floated together for a second, and Esme paddled over, but just as she reached them, and Fraser took her little hands in his, the dolphin leapt from the water, arched over them and dived in, nose-first, with barely a splash.

'Whoa!'

Esme's arms came up around his and Sara's shoulders as she floated between them. The trainer told them that the leap meant the dolphin liked them. It felt good, he thought. He liked it—the three of them together like this.

He tried to fight the nerves that kept striking while they swam and had their photos taken, and while Marcus filmed them on Esme's camera. Would all this still stay the same once Sara knew?

They were two days away from Florida. He wanted more of Sara's kisses. He wanted openness, and honesty, and to see the look on Esme's face when she discovered she was finally getting a new kidney—from her *real* father.

CHAPTER TWENTY-FOUR

'ARE YOU READY?'

'I still don't know where we're going.' Sara picked up her bag and slipped her ship ID into it, smiling up at him with glossed lips.

'That's because it's a surprise,' he said.

'You're very good at those,' she quipped, which made the ball of knots in his stomach tighten.

He wouldn't let it show.

He led them off the ship. The night was balmy and the port held a lingering smell of fruit and fried food as they made their way beyond the docks to the motorbike he'd hired. It had been the longest afternoon, knowing what he knew, but also knowing he had to wait for this moment.

'Another one of these?'

Sara frowned at the bike as he handed her a helmet. Her lilac dress fluttered around her wedge shoes. He was dressed in full-length khaki pants and a white shirt, slightly undone at the neck. They were both tanned now—another sign that their time on the ship was coming to an end.

'You'll be OK,' he said. 'You've swum with a dolphin, you've been water skiing alone, you've been up in a helicopter and you've saved a man from falling overboard…'

'I think you'll find *you* played a part in most of that.' Sara was smiling as he stepped towards her on the gravel path and helped her fasten the helmet. Palm trees swayed overhead.

'What I'm saying is, you've done a lot that you should be proud of, Cohen,' he told her.

'And so have you. Especially the Trevor thing. I'm glad Jasmine booked a flight home without him. We probably helped to change her life, you know. Hopefully for the better.'

'He told me that his father used to hit him,' he said now, studying her eyes under the night sky.

'So…like father like son?' she said with a sigh.

'Our fathers make us who we are, I suppose. For better or for worse.'

She seemed to contemplate his words, just as he was. He registered a flash of anger towards his own father, but he harnessed it to the breeze and sent it away. It wasn't the time for blame or comparisons; it never should be. He had Sara back now. And he had Esme too.

Guilt blew through him over blaming his father; for not being man enough himself to talk about his problems with Sara sooner.

She gripped his middle from behind as he drove them along the coast to the private beach of an expensive hotel, where they dined at a table so close to the sea that the waves almost lapped at their feet while they ate.

Lobster, prawns and rice served in scooped-out pineapple halves. Virgin mojitos and memories of their time together back in Edinburgh. They feasted on it all.

They talked about telling Esme about her upcoming surgery, and all the ways her life would change, but the waiting staff kept coming down to the beach to check on them, and it wasn't till their plates were cleared and the bill was paid that he could lead her across the sand to a quiet *cabana* and sit her down for their private conversation.

Sara's face in the moonlight showed blissed-out perfection as she nestled into the thick white cushions on a day bed surrounded on three sides by white linen curtains.

She was leaning back on both elbows, legs stretched out in front of her, eyes closed. The waves on the sand were a lullaby, even as nerves rattled him.

There was no more postponing the inevitable.

He turned her face to his. 'Do you even know how beautiful you are?' he said, and kissed her softly.

He slid his fingers around hers and trailed one thumb over her ring finger. When he pulled away she was still looking at their hands.

'Can you believe we're here now?' she said. 'I really thought you were going to break things off with me all those years ago, Fraser. I was so scared of being hurt by you that I hurt myself instead.'

He found himself swallowing back a lump in his throat. He put an arm around her on the cushions and breathed in the scent of her hair.

'I should have spoken to you about the stuff that was going on at the practice. And I *knew* my studies were suffering, and that I probably wouldn't pass the exams if I didn't get my head on straight, but I wanted to be there for you too.'

'*I* knew that I was holding you back; your dad was right about that even if it was brutal for me to hear it.'

He nodded sagely. 'And you wanted to be there for your family after your mum died. But I still think we both would have come to our senses and figured something out, Sara, if I hadn't come to London and seen you with *him*.'

She let out a sigh that he felt on his chest through his open shirt. 'Fraser, I can't believe you didn't say anything to me when you were there.'

He watched a crab scuttle along the sand. 'You'd made your decision—that's all I really saw,' he said. 'Then I just got on with things, Cohen—made my family happy. But if I'd known about Esme…' He paused.

Sara was facing him now. She reached a hand to his face.

'You couldn't have known I'd get pregnant with another man's baby,' she said. Her eyes were ringed with sorrow as she looked at him. 'Fraser, if you'd talked to me that day I might not have got pregnant by him at all.'

'Sara, listen…' He put a hand over hers, facing her on the cushions. This was the last time she'd look at him without knowing. He composed himself mentally, swept a clump of hair away from her eyes in the breeze. 'Sara, you *didn't* get pregnant with another man's baby.'

She was quiet. Her hand heated up under his and her cheeks began to flush. 'What are you talking about?' she said eventually.

'That's what this note says.' He pulled it out from his pocket—the one she'd picked up in his cabin. Her fingers were trembling as she took it. 'Esme and I have the same rare blood type,' he told her, watching her face. 'We're a perfect biological match.'

Sara shook her head. Her cheeks were redder than ever when he lifted her chin towards him.

'Sara, *we* are Esme's parents.'

'It can't be right.'

'The proof's right here.' He tapped the paper with his finger while she studied it in disbelief. Tears were glistening in the corners of her eyes. 'At first I thought you knew! I thought you were hiding it from me because you didn't want me as Esme's father, or didn't want *anyone* as her father. I'm sorry I hid it when I found out—but, honestly, I was in shock. It also was not the right time to have that conversation. I was going to wait until we got back to Florida, but...'

'This is crazy.'

He put a hand to the back of her hot neck, into her hair. 'It's good news if you want it to be,' he said.

'I didn't know,' she whispered, still shaking her head. 'You and I were always so careful with protection. I promise I wasn't keeping anything from you, Fraser—why would I do that?'

He moved the paper away and took her hands in his. 'I know. I believe you.'

'I thought she was *his*. Fraser, I *swear* it.'

'I said I believe you.'

She looking into his eyes through a wall of tears, the shock of discovery sinking in hard. He wrapped his arms around her shoulders, holding her small shaking frame tightly.

'You're really her father...' she breathed, sinking into him as they rested against the cushions. 'How could I not have known this?'

'How *could* you have known this?'

He held her tighter, allowing the weight of the truth to drift slowly from his shoulders. She hadn't got up. She wasn't angry. She was just shell-shocked—as he had been.

'I know you'll think there's a lot attached to this transplant now, with me being Esme's father,' he said, realising he had to reassure her. 'But I wanted to do this for Esme *before* I knew—it's how I found out. It's all I want if it's all *you* want. I won't come between you, or get in the way—'

'I'm so glad it's you, Fraser,' she said, cutting him off. Her fingers were latched in his hair. Her eyes were pooling. 'I mean, I'm thinking a thousand things, but the only one that matters is that I'm so glad *you're* her father. No matter what happens now, I mean that.'

'I'm glad it's me, too,' he told her.

And he was shocked at the water he felt in his eyes the moment the words left his lips.

CHAPTER TWENTY-FIVE

IT HAD BEEN inevitable that they'd made love that night, Sara mused, scooping a croissant from the buffet platter and putting it on her plate.

The final breakfast. The very last morning of the cruise. She'd come so far in so many ways it was almost unfathomable.

She'd been running over it for the past two days, while tending to her patients—re-dressing wounds, checking the eyes of a gentleman who'd smashed his glasses... The way she and Fraser had stayed glued to each other in that *cabana* for hours.

They'd been kissing to the sound of the rush of the Puerto Rican ocean—and talking, of course. Going over all the similarities between him and Esme, all the little things about her that now made sense, and all the things about her life and situation that hadn't...

'Mummy!'

Esme was calling to her from her seat next to Fraser. Sara watched the sunlight on his hair, saw how it fell on Esme's too, and lit her up even more. Father and daughter. It was still so overwhelming. She'd had no idea. No idea whatsoever in all this time.

Or had she?

She carried her plate across the deck towards them, contemplating all the times she'd been moved by something in Esme that had seemed familiar. So strangely familiar and yet she'd never quite been able to place it.

How quickly everything could change.

'How are you feeling?' he asked her now, pulling out her chair. He was wearing jeans and sneakers, like she was, ready to depart the ship.

'I'm OK,' she replied, but butterflies were swirling so hard inside her that she didn't even want her croissant.

They'd spent a night together in Fraser's cabin, unable to resist each other, but no one else was supposed to know that.

She was feeling the perfect mix of excitement, bewilderment, nervousness, anticipation and exhilaration all in one. She had an inkling that Esme would feel the same very soon.

They'd decided on the beach that night in Puerto Rico that they'd tell her Fraser was to be her donor when they got to Florida. Florida was now in sight.

'Esme, you know the cruise is almost over…' She picked up the croissant she knew she didn't want. 'Have you had a good time?'

Esme was beaming. 'Yes, Mummy, I've had the *best* time.'

Fraser folded his arms and turned to her in his chair. 'So have I. And you know what? Your mum and I have a surprise for you.'

Sara caught his glance and felt her heart somersault. Esme was pressing her hands together. Her eyes were like saucers.

The port was ahead, busy and green and surrounded by boats under blue skies. They'd have several hours once they docked to get their things off the ship, to say their goodbyes. She could tell that Esme would be sad to leave Jess and Marcus, but hopefully what they were about to tell her would make her feel better.

'Esme…' She lowered her voice and shuffled her chair closer. From the corner of her eye she saw Renee at the breakfast buffet, but in this moment she really didn't care *who* saw them.

'I know you like Dr Fraser,' she said, as her emotions bubbled up again, 'and it turns out he can do something incredibly special for you.'

Esme looked between them, intrigued. Fraser's support-ive hand was warm over Sara's now, and under the table his foot nudged hers. She took another nervous breath.

'Baby, it turns out that Fraser can be your donor. He can help you, Esme. He's a match! We found out on this trip.'

When the words were out, she realised how crazy they sounded, but Esme's big eyes had widened even further over her breakfast plate. She started jumping up and down in her seat with excitement.

'Really?' She was looking at Fraser in awe. Then look-ing back to Sara.

'I *can* help and I will,' Fraser told her. 'We just have to do some tests together—if you're OK with that?'

'I'm fine with that.'

The way she said it sounded so grown up for a five-year-old. She'd been through more in her five years than a lot of kids would go through in their entire lifetime. Sara put a hand to her soft hair as Esme climbed onto Fraser's lap and hugged him. It was a bear hug, and it made her heart soar when he returned it. *Now* she understood the bond be-tween them. Had they felt it, the two of them, without even knowing why?

'Do you know *why* Dr Fraser is such a good match for you?' she ventured now, as Esme settled on his lap and picked up some pineapple—her new favourite fruit.

'Because he likes making movies with me?'

Sara smiled. 'No, baby.'

'I'm a match because I'm your daddy,' Fraser said qui-etly, taking his cue. 'Is that a good enough surprise for you, Spielberg?'

Esme paused with her pineapple. A huge blast from the ship's horn shook Sara to the core. Florida had crept up on them even sooner than she'd anticipated it would.

'You're my daddy? My *real* daddy?' Esme looked de-lighted.

'Yes!' Fraser and Sara said at the same time.

Esme blinked a few times, wonderstruck. 'Why have I only just met you?'

Sara took her little hand. She'd been expecting this. 'It's complicated, and we'll tell you the whole story very soon. But for now you have to get ready to have some tests done in Florida.'

'Now? Today?'

'No time like the present,' Fraser said. 'We have to get my kidney over to you before the coral reef takes over.'

'Can we film it?' Esme asked, leaning back against his chest and nibbling her fruit, as if the news of her brand-new parent was old already.

'I don't know...'

'It would make the perfect ending to my film,' Esme coaxed, turning to him.

'You're going to make a great director one day,' he told her, putting his arms around her.

And there it was. Right there in their identical expressions when they grinned at each other. That strange feeling Sara had always felt was 'home' when she looked at Esme was all because of Fraser, and it had never even crossed her mind.

She shook her head, smiling ruefully.

'You look like a happy bunch,' Renee said, walking over and putting her hands on the back of Sara's chair. 'I'd like to thank you both personally for everything you've done on this trip. Did you have a good cruise, Esme?'

'The best—because I'm getting a new kidney *and* a new daddy,' she said bluntly, from Fraser's lap.

Sara felt her cheeks flaming once again. This was why they hadn't told Esme sooner; the whole ship would have known.

Renee's eyes said it all, though. She had known all along that something bigger was going on between them than general squabbles between exes, and she hadn't once pressured them. Sara was grateful. All the drama they'd been part of with Trevor and Jasmine had only served to highlight how special *their* relationship had always been, and she knew Renee could see that, too.

'I see. Well, that's great news,' Renee replied. There was genuine warmth in her eyes when she looked at Sara. 'I guess this is the start of a whole new journey, then. Will we see you all back next year?'

Fraser shrugged. So did Sara. She wasn't about to decide on that for definite yet, but in all honesty, after everything they had gone through on this cruise, she far preferred performing her medical duties on land.

Esme looked overjoyed as they ate and talked and said their goodbyes to everyone who came over to wish them well.

Sara couldn't stop looking at Fraser. For the last two nights she hadn't been able to get enough of him. His mouth and his tongue, his closeness, her legs wrapped around his middle. Their lovemaking was even more passionate than she remembered.

When they'd finally fallen into bed that night in Puerto Rico, after talking on the beach for hours, it had felt only right that they make love. And she had told him herself, when he'd been moving deep inside her, 'I always knew it felt right with you...'

They had no set plans beyond the transplant operation— not yet. But for the first time in a long time she didn't feel the need to make any. Somehow she knew in her heart that things would be OK.

CHAPTER TWENTY-SIX

'THIS IS QUITE a thing you've done—you should be proud of yourself.'

The kindly nurse was bustling about the room, and Fraser watched her place a vase of flowers by the bed and smiled at the familiar Scottish accent.

'Congratulations,' she said.

'Thanks, but it was really a no-brainer,' he said. 'I don't need two kidneys.'

He tried to sit up against the pillows, but the grey-haired nurse stopped him with a firm hand to his shoulder.

'Not yet.' She turned to rearrange the flowers and place the card he'd received from Boyd back upright. 'You might be sore for a couple of days, but I'm sure whatever discomfort you experience is for the greater good.'

'It definitely is.'

'Your daughter is the one you donated to?' She was smiling with her eyes. 'She's a lucky girl. You know what? My youngest nephew needed a kidney. He was water skiing on a family holiday just six weeks later. So a strong man like you should have no problem getting back to regular life— maybe even sooner than that.'

'Water skiing, huh?'

Fraser couldn't help feeling amused, even though he'd been slightly uncomfortable from the moment he'd arrived at the hospital. Not because of the surgery. That part didn't faze him. He'd have done anything to save his daughter's life, and the thought of having done so made his heart swell. He just wasn't used to being the patient.

'How's Esme doing?' He was anxious to see her—and Sara, of course.

'She's doing tremendously. Do you want me to take you to her?'

'I would love that.' He reached for the iPad on the bedside table, and the other items he'd brought along for this moment.

Fraser tried not to fidget with the IV and gauze as the nurse helped him into a wheelchair. The sight of himself in a blue gown was amusing, to say the least, as he was wheeled past the reflective windows in the hospital.

The surgery had gone to plan—as he had known it would in the hands of trusted friends and colleagues like Boyd—but there was one more somewhat elaborate plan he still had to put into action.

'What's on the iPad?' the nurse asked.

He smiled. 'Kind of a documentary,' he replied, sliding it against him down the side of the wheelchair.

It had all been go, go, go since they'd departed the *Ocean Dream* in Florida, and after the tests he and Esme had completed there had all verified that he was the perfect match for her, in every way, they'd opted to have the surgery performed in Scotland.

He'd had time to think since leaving the ship, about how back then, if he'd known Sara was pregnant with his child, he would have gone to the trustees and asked them outright to release the money. There would have been exceptional circumstances, after all. All their problems would have been fixed a lot sooner if his stupid pride hadn't been bruised by seeing her with another man.

He'd been alone for a few weeks with his thoughts while Sara had been preparing Esme for the operation back in London.

His mother had loved his plan to open a dialysis unit on the Breckenridge Practice premises. It had been hatching for a while in his head, and now she seemed to have found a new lease of life in planning a children's play area, and a special safe place for weary parents to gather and exchange tips on caring for kids on dialysis. It would bring more people to the surgery, and more expertise, more experience. Even more so if Sara and Esme joined him.

His stomach jumped inside. He could hear Sara's voice now.

She turned from Esme's bedside when the nurse swung the door open to her room. 'Fraser!'

Esme's small frame looked fragile in the bed. She smiled when she saw him. She was wearing pink pyjamas with a unicorn on the front.

Sara hurried to him and thanked the nurse, wheeling his chair to Esme's side. 'You're awake. How are you feeling?'

She leant in, dropping a light kiss on his lips, which he returned. Her eyes were shining. She looked well, as if years of worry had floated away, leaving her refreshed, reborn. Her hair brushed his face as she studied him up close.

'You look good to me,' she said, and smiled. 'Very good.'

'I feel good,' he said. 'I could murder a cheeseburger, though. How about you, Esme?'

'Am I allowed to eat those now?'

Sara sat on the side of the bed, ran a hand gently up Esme's small arm. 'I don't see why not—in a few days.'

'I'll have five—and some ice-cream,' Esme replied, matter-of-factly. 'I can eat what I want now I won't have to do dialysis, can't I?'

Fraser wanted to say something along the lines of *like father, like daughter*, but he didn't. He just reached for the iPad and pulled it out.

Sara looked suspicious, but she was almost smiling. 'What's that?'

'You haven't seen an iPad before?'

'Very funny.'

Sara looked tired, but beautiful as ever in a warm blue

woollen jumper, skinny jeans and black heeled boots. This was definitely not the Caribbean any more. She watched, intrigued, as he swiped the iPad and brought up a video.

'I hope you don't mind, but I have another surprise for you both,' he said.

He handed it to her and she held it between them so Esme could see. A lump formed in his throat as she pressed play. Seconds later she gasped, and Esme squealed in delight from the bed.

'You made another movie!'

'Your footage was just *so* good,' he replied, winking at her.

He studied their faces as they both took it in, and the words *my family* took root in his head.

Sara's hand kept flying over her mouth, as if she couldn't believe it. But it was all in there: a documentary, of sorts, of their time on the cruise. Stolen moments that Esme and Marcus had captured. A friend of Boyd's had helped him edit it, so the nights he'd had to spend without them hadn't seemed so long.

'Fraser, this is amazing!' Sara gushed, as Esme fought to hold the iPad in her hands.

There they were, he and Sara, swinging Esme between them on the deck of the ship. There they were again, dancing, looking into each other's eyes and laughing at something. There they were in the little boat with the water skis, and again on deck the night of the medevac. And with the dolphin at the aquarium.

Esme had captured it all—their togetherness—and he'd had it edited in the way he wanted Sara to remember it: the two of them falling slowly back together in spite of everything that had threatened to keep them apart.

He cleared his throat as another shot came up. Him, on the final day of the cruise, in his cabin. The sheets behind him were messed up, and only Sara would know why. He'd filmed this part himself.

'Sara, this has been one hell of a trip. And I want you to know that, whatever happens, I am and always will be madly in love with you—and with Esme too.'

His on-screen self was nervous. Fraser could hear it in his own voice.

'Now, please look at the real me, in front of you. I *hope* that's where I am!'

Sara looked up from the iPad as the picture of his on-screen self cut out. There in the hospital room Fraser pulled the tiny blue box from his pocket.

'I can't get down on one knee,' he said, holding out his hand to her from the wheelchair. 'But I can still say the words.'

She was shaking her head in disbelief.

'Sara Cohen,' he said, 'will you do me the utmost honour of marrying me?'

She sprang from the bed and dropped to her knees in front of the wheelchair. 'Oh, my…'

She trailed off as Fraser took her hand in his and held up the ring box, now open. Her eyes scanned the sparkling silver band and her mouth fell open at the practically blinking white diamond commanding attention at its centre.

'Yes!' she said, laughing through her tears, and Esme echoed her answer.

'Yes, yes, *yes*!' Esme squealed. 'Mummy, show me!'

Sara watched him slide the ring of her dreams onto her finger and took his face in her hands. 'I love you,' she whispered, up close. 'You have no idea how much.'

'Mummy, *show* me!'

Esme was adamant. Laughing, Sara stood up, but she kept one hand in Fraser's as she showed off her brand-new jewellery.

'It's so sparkly!' Esme was delighted.

Fraser's mother had helped him pick it, in the end. She was over the moon that they'd got back together—especially after hearing about everything that had happened—and was even more excited about having a granddaughter than he'd anticipated. She'd actually said she had never been so proud of him, and that, had he been there, his father would have been proud too.

'So, are you going to come to England and live with us?' Esme was looking at him now as if she had the whole thing planned out in her head already. 'Or are we going to live with you in Scotland?'

'I don't know what will happen yet,' he said honestly. 'Your mum and I still have to talk about some things. But...'

Sara was still staring at her ring. He hoped the giant diamond was everything she'd ever envisaged in an engagement ring. It was definitely what she deserved. And by the look on her face she was pleased.

'I'm setting up a dialysis centre on the Breckenridge Practice premises,' he said.

Sara's eyes sprang to his. She shook her head, as though everything was still sinking in.

'I want to create a safe place where kids can feel special, no matter what battles they're facing. And I want you to help me. And you too, Esme—you're my expert on this matter.'

'I get to help kids like me?'

Esme looked fascinated, and excited, just as he'd hoped. He envisaged a great life for them all in Edinburgh. There was plenty of room at the house, and in his central apartment—room for Sara's father too if he wanted to visit, or to stay.

Sara was looking at him in wonder, biting her bottom lip. 'You're amazing...' she said.

'It'll be a team effort,' he replied. 'But a fun one and a rewarding one, I hope. I couldn't sit back and not do everything in my power to help people like Esme. And Boyd's looking into funding...'

'It's a great idea,' she said. There was pure love and admiration in her eyes.

Esme was looking at him thoughtfully. 'Now that I have your kidney, you're a part of me.'

'That you are,' he told her fondly.

'And you *are* my daddy, so maybe I should call you Daddy.'

He couldn't help the smile that spread across his face. He wished he could stand up from the wheelchair, but he'd been instructed not to. 'What do you think, wife-to-be?' he asked Sara.

Her eyes told him she'd never thought she'd be sitting there, knowing Esme was safe and healthy at last, with a working kidney *and* a father.

'I think that would be fine by me,' she said after a moment. And when she kissed him again he didn't need words to know that she'd be moving to Edinburgh, and that their family would never be separated again.

'In that case, there's one more thing,' he said.

He reached behind him in the wheelchair and pulled out a bottle of champagne. Sara's eyes grew wide and flitted to Esme.

'Not for now.' He laughed, holding it out to her. 'Save it. It's for popping in your house—to mark this occasion. I figured you could finally make that extra cork mark on the ceiling.'

EPILOGUE

One year later

'THIS IS WHAT I used to call my robo-kidney!'

Esme was pointing the arm of her new toy stethoscope at one of the dialysis machines and Sara hurried over, unable to wipe the smile off her face. The centre had only been open a few months, but already Esme thought she ran the place. To be fair, she probably did.

'I see you're getting the full tour,' she said to the young boy in a blue tracksuit. He was hiding shyly behind his father.

'So this is the famous Esme,' the man said, shaking Sara's hand just as she registered the now all too familiar twinge of nausea starting to curl about her intestines and beyond.

She struggled not to let it show, casting her eyes to Fraser across the room.

'You used to be on dialysis?' the kid whispered, peeking out slightly, intrigued now.

This was the effect that Esme seemed to have on people. He was just seven, this boy who held the same look of uncertainty that Esme had used to hold in her eyes. It was his first time at the centre.

'I was, but my daddy gave me one of his kidneys,' Esme said proudly. Her chest seemed to swell in pride as she motioned to Fraser, who turned at the sound of the word 'daddy'. 'That's my daddy over there. He's the biggest hero for saving my life. Maybe we can find someone to give you a kidney too? But for now the robo-kidney will do the job for you. And I can tell you everything you need to know.'

Fraser smiled from across the room. He excused himself from the parents he was talking to by the weighing scales and made his way over. Sara's hand went automatically to her belly, as if the tiny seed inside her had registered his presence. She took a deep breath, willing the sick feeling to pass.

'Welcome,' Fraser said, shaking the man's hand.

His fingers brushed Sara's lower back through her jacket and Esme curled her arms around Fraser's waist. She looked up at him adoringly from between them.

'Thanks for coming,' Fraser went on. 'I see you've met our top kidney specialist.'

He lifted Esme easily into his arms and Sara's heart swelled at the sight of their faces pressed together for a second.

'She's six going on sixty,' he said, and Esme giggled.

Sara felted uncomfortable, and she looked at some charts, embarrassed. Fraser noticed.

'Are you OK,' he asked her as he put Esme down.

She nodded and moved her hand from her belly, aware of their patients again and of how ridiculously busy they were. He didn't know about the baby inside her yet—no one did.

Being pregnant now was probably bad timing. When they'd agreed to start trying for a baby shortly after the wedding she hadn't actually expected it to happen so soon. They had only been married six months. She hadn't even allowed herself to get excited yet.

They continued the tour together, Fraser and Esme, while Sara administered dialysis to an Iranian man who'd moved from Glasgow to a village nearby, just to come here. Pride flowed through her as she took in the magnitude of all that they'd achieved in such a short amount of time.

They were well on track to becoming the second largest kidney care provider in the UK, with more machines than anywhere else in Scotland. A growing number of patients of all ages and backgrounds were signing up, having heard about the experienced husband-and-wife team, plus their adorable daughter, who were running it.

They could accommodate up to three shifts of patients a day now, and had patients visiting three times a week for four hours or more. Most people knew Esme by now, and if she wasn't there they'd ask for her—especially the kids.

It had been Esme's idea to bring a 'wall of fame' to Edinburgh, too. It was where each kid shared a little information about their lives outside of dialysis.

'We used to have one of these in London, where I got my dialysis treatments,' she was saying now, pointing at the photos of kids' faces, each one in the centre of a colourful paper flower.

Without the dialysis herself, Esme was even more vibrant and playful—and perpetually excited about new adventures and ice-cream.

Sara wondered yet again how she'd feel about her latest news.

She glanced at Fraser as another twinge of nausea struck. She gripped the desk quickly, and one of the biomedical technicians—a lady called Liz—put a hand on her arm to steady her.

'Mrs Breckenridge? Are you OK?'

'I'm OK, thank you,' she said, but she knew her face was probably too pale.

Liz frowned and lowered her voice. 'Let me take over. Maybe you should go and lie down? Someone in your condition shouldn't be on her feet so much.'

Sara gaped at her in surprise. Liz pulled an imaginary zip over her lips, and winked at her before taking over her duties.

Unable to stop the nausea now, Sara stepped aside quickly, into the water treatment room. Taking long, deep breaths, she leaned against the huge cool tank, waiting for it to pass.

'Sara?'

When she opened her eyes Fraser was closing the door to the room and stepping towards her under the glaring sterile lights.

'I saw you come in here—what's the matter?'

She swallowed, aware that she probably looked terrible.

'You look green,' he confirmed, putting a big hand to her forehead. 'Here, sit down.'

He pulled a chair away from the wall and motioned for her to sit, but she stayed pressed against the cool tank. It was making her feel better.

She closed her eyes, still sucking in breaths as Esme's high-pitched voice carried in from the treatment room.

'Fraser, I'm pregnant,' she said, putting a hand to her belly again.

His eyes widened in front of her. He stared at her in total shock for a moment.

'I know there's a lot going on,' she continued, 'with this place and with Esme, but…'

'Why didn't you tell me?' Fraser's look of shock was transformed into one of pure exhilaration. 'Sara, this is… This is really good news. I think… Don't you?' He put his hands to her shoulders and stared deep into her eyes. 'You *are* excited, aren't you?'

'I am,' she told him. 'I *am*. I just know how busy we are…'

'Family comes first,' he said firmly. 'You know that.'

'I do,' she said, feeling silly now.

She'd known he'd be excited. Slowly but surely, she allowed herself to feel excited too. The look on his face meant everything to her.

He ran his hands through his hair. 'Wow… I'm going to be a dad again—really?'

He pulled her close and she sighed with relief into the skin of his warm neck. Her nausea was fading, thankfully, and in its place was a new set of butterflies. He'd *always* given her butterflies.

'How long have you known?' he asked.

'A couple of weeks,' she said. 'I wanted to be absolutely sure before I told you. Are we ready for this?'

'Of course we're ready for this. 'You know, I *should* have known,' he told her now, stepping back and smiling at her mischievously.

'Because of all the hot sex we've been having?' she whispered, raising an eyebrow.

He grinned. 'No! Well, yes, but mostly because of *this*.'

Fraser reached into the pocket of her white coat and swiftly pulled out her knitting needles, still laced into a ball of pale blue wool.

'Click, click, click,' he teased, smiling as he held them out.

She snatched them back, laughing. 'One pink mitten, one blue mitten—just in case,' she told him, shoving her work in progress back into her pocket. 'Seriously, Fraser, are you ready for this?'

She scanned his blue eyes, looking for any trace of doubt. She saw none.

'We have help,' he said. 'We have money, we have time, and we have this house. We have Esme. Sara, we are *all* ready.'

He brought her fingers to her lips before he kissed her up against the water tank. She prayed no one would open the door.

'I think we need to get some more champagne,' he said after a moment against her lips, 'and some ice-cream.'

'Ice-cream?'

'Isn't that how Esme celebrates all her good news now? I happen to think she's going to be crazy for a new brother or sister.'

'As crazy as I am about you?'

Sara wrapped her arms around her husband. Seven years and a daughter had brought them to this point, and in a few more months they'd be a family of four.

She had no idea what lay ahead, but she'd try to stay true

to the promise she'd made herself and Fraser…that every day would be an adventure that they'd cherish, no matter how stormy the ride.

* * * * *

LET'S TALK

Romance

For exclusive extracts, competitions
and special offers, find us online:

- 🅕 facebook.com/millsandboon
- 🅞 @millsandboonuk
- 🅨 @millsandboon

Or get in touch on 0844 844 1351*

For all the latest titles coming soon,
visit millsandboon.co.uk/nextmonth